BLACK HEART BOYS' CHOIR

CURTIS M. LAWSON

FOREWORD BY S. T. JOSHI

A WYRD HORROR BOOK

BLACK HEART BOYS' CHOIR

COVER ART BY CARRION HOUSE

ISBN: 9781075108068

CURTIS M. LAWSON

DEDICATION

To Robb Kavjian, who walked the razor's edge with me, and to Louis Boulanger, who helped keep me from falling off.

ACKNOWLEDGEMENTS

My deepest and most sincere thanks to S. T. Joshi for his support and guidance, Gregor Xane, Andrew Boylan, and Robb Kavjian for serving as sounding boards, and to Christine and Tristan for their love and patience.

FOREWORD

The fusion of music and weirdness has been a slim but consistent thread in literary history. H. P. Lovecraft's "The Music of Erich Zann" (1922) is perhaps the best-known example today, but there are many others, ranging from J. Meade Falkner's *The Lost Stradivarius* (1895) to Algernon Blackwood's *The Human Chord* (1910). E. T. A. Hoffmann (1776–1822) was both a composer and an author of weird fiction, his work was the basis— partial or complete—of such musical works as Tchaikovsky's *The Nutcracker,* Offenbach's *Tales of Hoffmann,* and Wagner's *Tannhäuser* and *Die Meistersinger.* Hoffmann wrote an opera based upon *Undine,* the short novel published in 1811 by his friend Friedrich Heinrich Karl, baron de La Motte-Fouqué; but it does not appear as if he incorporated musical elements into his own weird tales. From a very different perspective, rock bands of all sorts have drawn inspiration from Lovecraft and other authors of supernatural fiction, in ways both hackneyed and creative.

Now Curtis M. Lawson has, in *Black Heart Boys' Choir,* created a mesmerising tale of music and terror that can take rank with any of its predecessors. The supreme difficulty of writing about music is, of course, the utter divergence of the two media;

perhaps the divergence is a bit less extreme in the case of vocal music, since such works are manifestly designed to appeal both to the musical and to the verbal imagination. Even so, as any music critic can tell you, trying to describe the effects of a musical composition by means of words is often a hopeless task. And yet, Lawson has created a striking narrative that brings to life the latent terror of a piece of music that may have the potential to tear apart the fabric of creation.

But there is a great deal more going on in Lawson's narrative than the horror of a possibly supernatural musical composition. His portrayal of high school life, with its inevitable cliques, bullying, and personal traumas (academic, sexual, and otherwise), is both grim and poignant, and many will be able to relate to his depiction of a cadre of loners and outsiders who seek the ultimate revenge on their rivals. The central figure in the text, Lucien Beaumont, reveals the many sides of his conflicted personality through his own words, carrying the reader on in appalled fascination as he advances (or descends) into psychosis.

I myself sing in a community choir—the Northwest Chorale, in Seattle—and have composed both instrumental and vocal music, so I received a particularly powerful jolt from *Black Heart Boys' Choir*. But no knowledge of music is needed to appreciate this skillful novel; all one needs is an

awareness of the torments that beset many youths in this land, and an appreciation of the spectacular violence of which they are capable.
—S. T. JOSHI

CURTIS M. LAWSON

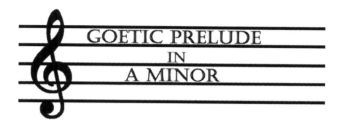

GOETIC PRELUDE
IN
A MINOR

The end of the world, in my experience, is a microcosmic event. It is an intimate experience rather than the cold and dry ultimate chapter in history. Armageddon is not a pandemic wiping out mankind; it is one man's illness driving him to a makeshift gallows. Ragnarok is not a final war but the pain and fear of a single soldier bleeding out, far from home. And divine retribution is not the indiscriminate flooding of a world but personal, up-close violence against the guilty.

The end of the world, as it expresses itself at this place and in this time, is set to music. My choir sings as one, and bodies fall around us, each a universe unto itself, now forever extinguished. Brimstone hail rips through arteries and organs. Our voices shatter bone and coax blood from every orifice. All the while Amduscias, rising from the burning pit below, greedily sups upon death.

If this night is remembered, history will judge it as a mass tragedy of nameless victims, but it is so much more than that. Each death, when you think of it, is cosmic in proportion. For every microcosm destroyed, a shockwave echoes out across familial bonds and through the collective consciousness of man, wreaking havoc across countless vistas of reality.

The ashes of our sheet music blow across the floor, but with each drop of blood and every scream Amduscias, our infernal conductor, reveals a new note. We are not immune to the disastrous hymn we sing. Burning hail tears at our flesh and shreds our insides, but our voices stay strong. No one sings too sharp or flat. No one loses time. They've come such a long way, my choir.

Richard Wagner once proposed the construction of a theater on the Rhine for the performance of his Ring cycle. The four operas, performed on consecutive nights, would be concluded with the theater in flames. A perfect cadence.

Like Wagner's dream, our final theater is in flames. Disco lights and the amber glow of hellfire refract through stagnant water wept from iron pipes above. The sprinklers are impotent against the inferno, but the droplets glow, like hellish faeries, adding a deeper layer of theatricality to our performance.

Our victims flee in rudderless panic. They trample the dead and dying, all pretense of virtue and morality squashed beneath the threat of oblivion. I hope that a few among them might look around before their deaths and see themselves as I do—a gathering of vermin—a writhing ratking.

Ari Cole's face explodes, and bloody tears of

satisfaction roll down my cheeks. One note resolved. Asher, our fearless percussionist, falls dead upon his final snare hit of the crescendo. His death howl is another note brought into discord.

F, twice below middle C, accompanies my sustained D sharp, and I feel some organ burst behind my ribs. I'm dying. Of that there is no doubt. The song is nearly complete, however, and I will sing until this body fails. Even as the reaper's scythe teases my face, I have no fear. I shall be immortal in my art, the best parts of me captured in stave and song. Neither death nor Hell can undo that magic.

Soon Amduscias, my muse and betrayer, will try to sup upon my synaptic end. He will find nothing, though, but a dead, black heart. My world ended years ago, long before this night of victory and suffering. And that's what this story is really about, isn't it? How one person's suffering can amplify and resonate like a song shared with the world.

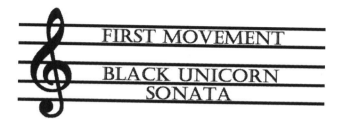

CHAPTER 1

The first fifteen years of my life speed before my vision. Most of it is inconsequential humdrum, alongside minor tragedies and snippets of happiness, though I'm able to pick out highlights here and there.

My father singing to me as a baby and a toddler.

My first day of school.

A family trip to Manhattan.

The day my father stopped singing.

The rest goes by in a dizzying blur of sights, sounds, and smells. The juniper smell of gin. The hook from a Beethoven piece. A sunset over the Boston skyline. Then time dilates, and I find myself at the end of this past summer.

Is this where it all began? The beginning of the end for Enfield, Massachusetts? Is this the moment we began our death march? Or was it further back still? When Gravetree and my father, like the musical equivalents of John Dee and Edward Kelley, uncovered *The Madrigal of the World's End*? Or maybe in the ancient days when Amduscias stood beside Lucifer and took up arms against God

Almighty?

It's inconsequential, I suppose. This is the time that my mind has brought me to.

My mother has just about drunk away all the money that Father left us, and royalty checks for his recordings are both meager and inconsistent. We both have to make sacrifices if we are to get by, or so I'm told. That means moving out of our big house on Raylene Street and acclimating to a two-bedroom condo across town that can't accommodate Father's baby grand.

With the move comes a change of schools. The Academy was putting too much of a dent into our dwindling savings, which means my senior year will be spent at Swift River High—a drab public school full of students with drab aspirations.

As for Mother, the profit from the equity from the house on Raylene Street. allows her to maintain her diet of wine and pills without the burden of looking for a job, so I suppose all she needs to sacrifice is my last bit of respect for her. Yes, she is losing the big house too, but it's not as if she ever leaves her bedroom.

I don't plan on sticking around after graduation. I'm thinking I'll go to New York and seek out some of Father's contacts, but Chicago or even London aren't out of the question. Even if I only move as far as Boston proper, though, I'll need a good chunk of money, come June.

There's a record store in town, one of the only tidbits of culture in Enfield, and I convince the owner to give me a summer job. It doesn't pay much, which was understandable. Customers rarely come in, but those who do are mostly bearable. It's older folks mainly—post-college hipsters, elderly jazz aficionados, and some scumbag named Leo who buys house music with the money he makes selling dope outside a nearby gas station. The slim body of customers often comment on my precocious charm, though using the word precocious for a sixteen-year-old strikes me as a bit condescending.

I often wonder how the owner, an old hippie named Jonas, manages to keep the lights on. The financials of the record store aren't my concern, however, and a rarity of customers suits me just fine. It gives me a chance to be out of our tiny condo with the broken air conditioners and away from my mother. It's usually slow enough that I can spend most of my day doodling portraits of my favorite composers and daydreaming of joining their ranks. Also, I'm surrounded by music. Sure, most of it is pop trash from some bygone generation or another, but Jonas occasionally lets me play what I like, and I uncover a few gems. The soundtrack to *A Clockwork Orange,* featuring two movements from Beethoven's Ninth. *Das Rheingold,* conducted by Sir Georg Solti. Sir John Eliot Gardiner's rendition of the *Mass in B minor*.

Although the store caters almost exclusively to adults, the occasional high school student pops in. I know most of them only by face. All my friends are from the Academy, so I never bothered socializing in my hometown. Nevertheless, they all seem to know me. They walk the aisles of the shop, talking in Irish whispers about my family's misfortune.

"Jenny, look. It's that weird kid who always

wears a suit."

The CD I'm swapping out of the stereo snaps in my hands.

"I heard his whole family is nuts, and he goes to some school for like really troubled kids."

I hold two jagged crescents. They shine with chromatic brilliance.

"My mom said his dad killed himself, and his mother blew through all their money. I guess they had to sell that big house on Raylene. That must be why he's working here."

I dive across the counter, on top of Jenny. She screams, and her breath is hot and sweet on my face. I snatch her tongue between two fingers and saw through it with the serrated edge of a broken, dollar-bin Mozart CD.

When they finish their gossip and their browsing they usually leave without buying anything. Either that or they make a pretentious show out of purchasing some shitty, flower-child bullshit. How fucking deep they think they are for listening to their grandparents' pop music!

There is one kid my own age, however, who comes in on a regular basis. His name is Maxwell Sirois, and he's not too terribly obnoxious, nor is he interested in the gossip around my family name. While the rest of our peers consume disposable singles on iTunes, Maxwell prefers full albums on disc and vinyl. He appreciates the arrangement of songs and the totality of albums as a work of art. We talk about this quite a bit. Jonas sometimes argues against this, pointing out the importance of old 45s that predate the concept of the EP, but we never pay him much mind.

What's more, Maxwell does not pollute his ears nor his mind with pop music. His tastes are odd and varied but show a level of thought, mostly choral music, soundtracks, and something called dungeon synth, which varies from intriguing to miserable.

Over the course of the summer, we become friends. He's more outgoing than I am and has a quick-witted charm, but he's self-deprecating and lacks confidence. His wardrobe is an unremarkable collection of baggy T-shirts and shorts meant to camouflage his considerable girth along with the unique nature of his interests and personality.

Maxwell takes me to his secret spots around town, places that no one else knows about or bothers with—old storm sewers, rotten piers, and abandoned train yards. Anywhere he can get away from the mindless teenage socialites and bullies of Enfield. They're all forgotten, decrepit places, but each holds a sort of melancholy beauty.

When we get bored of Maxwell's secret places we usually go to my house, partly because my mother leaves us alone, but also because I can use the help getting things in order around the condo. Mother is content living out of unpacked boxes for eternity, so the burden falls to me to create some semblance of a home. This is fine. Her lack of interest in anything outside of the four walls of her bedroom means that I can utilize the living room space for my own musical pursuits.

Maxwell and I set up bookshelves, which we fill with what books of my father's that I had saved—a mix of his own compositions, sheet music for various piano concertos, treatises on musical theory, and biographies of great composers. We roll an old and poorly tuned piano (a concession prize from my mother for turning my life upside down) against the largest wall, directly next to a window that sees little direct sunlight. In lieu of a television as the centerpiece of the room (Mother has annexed that to her bedroom), we set up my Mac and rack system, along with hooks to store cables.

Decorations consist of a few family photos, back from the days when we were a family, and some early Impressionist prints. My mother insisted we keep them. Monet was a passion she shared with Father, though I don't care for Impressionism myself. I find the ambiguous dimensions of the flurried brush strokes unsettling and eerily true to the uncertainty of life.

Maxwell gives me a bobblehead of Ludwig van Beethoven as a housewarming gift. It sits atop my piano. Its frivolity is out of place in the room, but it brings a smile to my face. Its silly, plastic dimensions are an apt, if depressing, reminder of my place in the world. A teenage intellectual marooned in a blue-collar wasteland—a disposable, white trash Beethoven.

CHAPTER 2

It's the first day of school, and the hours are ticking by in slow motion. It hits me that I have not been without music all summer, not for more than a minute or two. Whether it be from records playing at work, composing and practicing at home, or concertos and symphonies streaming through my PC speakers, I have shunned silence and the uncomfortable thoughts it chauffeurs.

It's the first day of school, and I find myself anxious, not because I'm sitting across from the guidance counselor but for the lack of crying piano strings or whispering woodwinds.

"You know there isn't a dress code," she says, trying to start things off with a joke. I straighten my tie, black silk with diagonal white stripes, and tell her that I'm aware.

She laughs at this, even though there was no humor in my voice, then gestures to herself.

"I guess I'm one to talk," she jokes, pointing out her drab khaki-colored pantsuit. There's a pause where she waits for me to laugh or smirk, but I don't, and her smile straightens a bit.

"I know you've been through a lot these past

few years, Lucien. Losing your father, adjusting to a new home and lifestyle, and now a new school on top of it. I get that it's tough."

The guidance counselor's name is Ms. Kane. She's a middle-aged woman who speaks like a television therapist, her voice a patronizing mixture of measured calm and bartered sympathy.

I nod, wondering how she knows so much about me already. She answers without my having to pose the question, my thoughts apparently plain on my face.

"Mr. Larson at Birch Creek wrote us a letter. He was concerned about how you might adjust and hoped someone might reach out to you."

Mr. Larson is the Headmaster of Birch Creek Academy. A stern man yet sharp and artistic. Not as brilliant as my father but far more disciplined and effective. He would often affirm that a real man was like a perfectly balanced blade, and I can think of no better way to describe him.

We formed something of a bond during my time at the Academy. He had a passing interest in opera and oversaw the school choir, which kept us in one another's company quite often. It would seem that our bond was only as strong as my mother's purse strings, however, as I was banished once our funds ran dry.

"Swift River High doesn't offer the same degree of special support that you're accustomed to," Ms. Kane says, seeming to choose her words carefully. "But I'm here to talk if you ever need to, for any reason."

I thank her, hoping that this might mark the

end to our meeting. She continues on, however, asking if I've made any friends in the school, dashing my hopes for release. I tell her that I've made friends with Maxwell Sirois, and her spirits visibly lighten.

"Max is such a wonderful kid, and he's interested in music as well, I believe. Isn't he?"

Again, I find it curious how much she knows about me. Did Mr. Larson mention my passion for music in his letter? Is she familiar with my father and his work and just assumes my interests are similar?

"You should try out for the glee club!" she cries. "The both of you."

A sour expression possesses my face. "Glee club?" I ask.

"Oh, you'll love it! They do really fun renditions of popular songs. It's not some geeky barbershop quartet stuff."

"I suppose the school doesn't have a proper choir?"

It's the first day of school, and Ms. Kane is telling me that glee club and choir are practically the same thing.

The rest of the day is a haze.

I'm in third-period American Literature. A pretentious teacher in a cheap brown suit that almost perfectly matches his skin tone is writing his name on the board and discussing the dreadfully predictable syllabus. *I snatch a lighter from the burnout next to me, set flame to my copy of* The Scarlet Letter, *and encourage Mr. Jackson to get more creative with the curriculum.*

I'm at lunch, and I meet Ari Cole for the first time. He feigns interest in my tie before dipping it into his ketchup. *As he laughs I swing my lunch tray up into his jaw and his teeth slam together, shattering like hammered porcelain.*

I'm in last-period AP Chemistry with Maxwell. He's wearing a Walmart knockoff of my outfit—a white Van Heusen dress shirt with a polyester tie and ill-fitting slacks. It's nice to see him at least trying to dress a bit better, but it provokes the rabble. They want the bar set low, and they lash out at anyone who attempts to raise it. One of them calls out from the seat behind us, asking if we're dressed up for our wedding. *I turn to our heckler, place one hand against his jawline and lean into to kiss him. When I pull away his severed lip is between my teeth.*

The final bell rings.

Maxwell and I are carried along in the stream of students as we emerge from last period to my locker. I place the books I won't need on the high shelf, next to my bobblehead Beethoven who has found a new home there, amongst ink and crayon sketches of Wagner and Hadyn. I compliment Maxwell on his outfit, as well as I can bring myself to. It's cheap, off-the-shelf stuff, but it's a step up from the oversized T-shirts and cargo shorts he'd worn all summer.

Something across the hall catches Maxwell's attention. I close my locker and follow him to a flyer for glee club tryouts. There is an excitement in his eyes that is almost embarrassing to witness. He reads my judgment and downplays his interest.

"It's kind of gay, but it's the only music program left in school."

The flyer depicts cartoonishly pretty figures, their open O mouths spewing random eighth and quarter notes. I find myself without words.

"At least it will look good on a college résumé," Maxwell says, "and it might get us out of a class or two."

College is not part of my escape plan. It's a sucker's bet, but I don't bother getting into my feelings on higher academia. Instead, I find myself moved by the thought of escaping one or two of the unintentionally remedial classes that Swift River High offers.

"I'll consider it."

CHAPTER 3

It's Labor Day weekend, and Maxwell and I have orchestra seats at Boston Symphony Hall. He's dressed in the same shirt and slacks he wore to school the other day, but I've given him one of my ties. I couldn't bear the thought of him wearing polyester to the symphony. He jokes about the tie, which is skinnier and more fashionable than his own broad, *church on Sunday* ties.

"Fat guy with a skinny tie," he sings in his impressive countertenor. Some say that the ability to laugh at oneself is a virtue. I fear Maxwell's self-deprecation is rooted deeper than good-natured humor, though.

Looking around the concert hall, it seems that my concern over the quality of Maxwell's tie is misplaced. The standard of dress has clearly deteriorated since my last visit. Polo shirts and tan khakis speckle the crowd, like ever-increasing liver spots on society's aging flesh.

Everywhere I look, even in these hallowed walls, Western civility seems to recede. The man in front of us is sixty if he's a day yet couldn't be bothered to throw on so much as a button-up shirt.

What kind of example does that set?

Father always wore a suit, even to breakfast. It was, he explained, a man's duty to himself always to look his best. Mr. Larson from the Academy was of much the same mind, often citing that a suit commanded respect and showed it in turn. If more people did both of those things on a regular basis the world would be a much better place, I'd wager.

The conductor takes the stage and, after a brief applause, the crowd hushes. His name is Philip Gravetree, a colleague of my father. There is an air of madness about him. His white hair, a wild mess atop his head, stands in stark contrast to the neatness of his tuxedo. His head darts around, surveying the crowd. He twitches and flinches at the space around him and at the silence of the hall. I remember him being odd on the occasions we had met, but not neurotic. Madness often takes up residence in the gifted, however, so I shouldn't be surprised.

Tonight Gravetree is conducting Gorecki's *Symphony of Sorrowful Songs.* He was thoughtful enough to send tickets for Mother and me. Since she ventures no further from her room than the refrigerator or bathroom, I naturally offered the extra ticket to Maxwell.

Gravetree waves a conductor's wand and the double bass swells from nothing, introducing the first bars of the piece. His unease evaporates, leaving herculean confidence in its place. I am affected in a similar fashion. The world vanishes as the music kisses my ears. All problems and anxieties crumble beneath the bassy vibrations, leaving my soul light and free.

The shabbily dressed old man in front of us is bleeding from his ears. Gravetree gestures with his other hand, and cellos join in. *Their tone shatters the codger's skull like glass beneath a hammer. Skull fragments and cerebral flotsam patter against Maxwell and me like warm, soothing rain. I take joy in the sensation. Maxwell seems indifferent, hypnotized by the music.*

Aside from being a talented conductor, Gravetree is an excellent composer. He and Father were mutual admirers of each other's compositions, and I recall that they had begun a collaboration left unfinished in the wake of my father's death. I wonder if whatever he and Gravetree had been working on together might have survived.

The performance, all three movements, fills the better part of an hour. Fifty-three minutes of pure emotion. I'm enraptured by each morose counterpoint and every movement of Gravetree's wand. Tears wash freely down my face. Some find crying a shameful thing, but I never have.

The performance ends. The crowd rises, myself and Maxwell included, and we all applaud. Gravetree stands still with his head lowered. His shoulders rise and fall as if the mere act of breathing is taking great effort. After the space of a few seconds, all the confidence and power I had seen in him while conducting are gone. His head is pointed downward as he exits the stage, his back slouched. The spasms, so prevalent before the performance, return. His mouth is moving, though his mutterings are lost to us.

I consider trying to get backstage so that I

might thank Gravetree for the tickets and perhaps request a letter of introduction for when I seek out work after graduation. I decide against this, given his strange behavior on stage. It might be more prudent to write a letter, so as not to strain his anxiety further.

We make our way to North Station, choosing to walk the distance in lieu of dealing with the obnoxious throngs of barflies and clubgoers we might encounter on the subway. There we'll catch the commuter rail back to Enfield.

Even though we manage to avoid the idiot weekend revelers on the Green Line, dregs, schemers, and addicts call to us from the gutters and doorways. Some beg for money; others demand it. Walking down Tremont Street we ignore them, chatting and enjoying the high that the symphony has left us with. "Cheap fucking queers!" one of them yells out as we pass. I turn back to see her, a skeleton of a woman with stringy red hair, huddled in the doorway to a McDonald's. "Keep walking, faggots!"

I gesture for Maxwell to pause and stroll back to the wretched she-thing. She sneers at me and spits with derision. With Gorecki's genius still echoing in my mind, I kick her in the teeth, as hard and as fast as I can. She cries out, blood and bits of broken, rotten incisors dripping down her chin. The sole of my brogue slams into her face again and again, in perfect metronome timing, until a crimson waterfall is cascading from her open, ruined mouth. Content that she will harass no one else, I rejoin Maxwell.

We get to North Station and board a ten o'clock train. It pulls out of the station, leaving the beauty of Boston proper behind, and I immediately feel the suffocating gravity of Enfield pulling us back.

Maxwell and I find seats, and we discuss the history of Gorecki's Symphony. The seed for the piece had been a commission to commemorate the Holocaust. Gorecki would later say that the finished work was about general suffering in a universal sense, rather than sorrow tied to a specific event.

"I think he was right to distance the piece from the Holocaust," I explain. "In a thousand years what happened at Auschwitz and Dachau will be a footnote in history, no more important than the hundred genocides that came before or the hundred that will come about as history continues to unfold."

Maxwell's face goes white. He mutters in a hushed tone that I shouldn't undermine the tragedy of the Holocaust.

"I'm not," I say. "I'm simply stating that Gorecki's work, unfettered by the bonds of historical context, will be a testament to human sorrow for time immemorial."

"Don't you think remembering what those people went through and warning against it happening again is more important than worrying that a piece of music might feel dated in a thousand years?"

"No," I answer, stricken by the oddness of his question.

There is a moment of silence where Maxwell stares at me as if he's trying to take measure of my soul. He blinks and looks down at his phone, leaving me to wonder what he saw. Or maybe what he didn't see.

Staring at his screen, Maxwell changes the subject. He asks about my father's connection to Gravetree and their collaborations together. I share with him what I know, and we decide to look through my father's remaining notes and songbooks for some trace of their shared work when we get back to Enfield.

It's still too early for the bar crowd to be leaving Boston, so the train ride is uneventful, aside from my anxiety growing with every mile closer to home. Around Leominster, I find trouble breathing. By Gardner I'm nauseous. As we pass Prescott Lake my heart is beating with a *prestissimo* tempo. Each little burb, growing smaller and increasingly claustrophobic, is a reminder of my bondage to Enfield until next June.

June will never come for me, of course, but I don't know that yet.

"Enfield Depot!" the conductor cries as the train slows to a stop. Maxwell has fallen asleep. I shake him awake, and we step off the train into the small, suburban night.

The condo is dark when we arrive. An open jar of instant coffee sits on the counter, and a pot of oil clouded water on the stovetop. Mother was up and about at some point and left me with her mess, as usual.

I dump the pot into the sink, and the stink of hot dogs wafts up from the water as it circles the drain. The smell makes me sick to my stomach. I bring the coffee grounds close to my face and inhale its strong, bitter aroma, exorcizing the Oscar Meyer smell from my sinuses.

The cheap Dollar Store coffee makes me long for the smell of Father's tea. Black, French Vanilla in the morning and peppermint before bed. Those were wonderful smells.

Maxwell pulls two plastic cups from the cabinet and a bottle of tonic water from the fridge. He fills the cups halfway with seltzer and ice, as I retrieve a bottle of Bombay Sapphire I keep hidden beneath the couch. Not that Mother would care if she caught us drinking. She's far too progressive and deeply broken to care about such things. No, I keep it hidden so that she won't drink it herself.

Like vanilla and mint teas, the juniper smell of gin was a staple of our house on Raylene Street. Father would have a shot after dinner each night, and his breath was always warm with it as he'd send me off to bed with a hug.

With our drinks in hand, we retire to the living room and search through the bookshelves. I know Father's published works inside and out, so we focus on his notes and handwritten songbooks. Most of what we find are studies, exercises, and worksheets. Transcriptions of major key songs turned minor and vice versa. Short tone poems of his favorite myths and fictions. Fugues designed around the simple melodies of rock songs but expanded into so much more.

The notes on the pages come to life in my head, and I can almost hear Father's tenor voice singing them. I close my eyes, and I can see him, the memory aided by the smell of gin, so clear in my mind. His eyes are full of passion and vitality. Another voice calls out, but it's lost beneath my father's song.

The other voice speaks louder this time, and my mind goes dark, save for a spotlight centered on a well-dressed man swinging from a rope. Father's voice cuts out, his throat crushed by a slipknot.

I open my eyes, and I'm back in the shitty little condo that Mother and I share. The unhome where Father has never been. Maxwell is waving a songbook in front of me.

"Earth to Lucien! Is this gin kicking your ass, man?"

"Huh?" I ask with a flurry of blinks.

"I think I found the piece your dad did with Gravetree. It's all fucked up, though."

I reach for the songbook. It's a plain, unassuming thing, bearing much wear. A cheap, spiral-bound notebook with pre-printed staves on each page. Scrawled in permanent marker across the manila cover is the inscription: *Madrigal of the World's End. By Louis Beaumont and Philip Gravetree.*

"What do you mean, it's all fucked up?" I ask.

"Open it," Maxwell implores, looking more than a bit forlorn.

I turn back the cover, and what I see hits me like a brick to the face. A time signature of 4/4 is clear next to the treble and baritone clefs, as are the words *Goetic Prelude in A minor,* but almost every note, on every bar, is covered in strokes of black ink.

The stray whole note or paired eighths have managed to survive unmarred, but the first page of the prelude is unreadable.

The next page is the same, as is the one after that—smears of black ink with only occasional notes escaping oblivion. It's clear where one movement ends and another begins, but little more is legible.

The pages after the second movement are missing. Someone has torn them out. I remove a perforated bit of paper from the binding and hold it up for Maxwell to see.

"I suppose my mother ran out of ink."

"You think your mom did this?" Maxwell asks with genuine surprise.

How charmed my dear friend's life is that he cannot begin to imagine a wife and mother doing something as insane and despicable as erasing her dead husband's legacy. I can imagine it all too well. It plays out in my mind, Mother in a manic fit after taking too many uppers in an attempt to even out, brushing India ink over Father's genius. I can see her making wild, slashing movements as if she were a frenzied artist desperate to empty her mind into the world, rather than a vandal erasing the thoughts and passions of others.

"What can be done?" I ask, more to myself than Maxwell.

He takes a sip of his gin and tonic and leans back in silence. I'm too angry to remain sitting, and instead of a sip I take a hard swallow, finishing off the cup. Without much thought, I march into the kitchen and pour myself another drink before I start fishing through the junk drawer in search of an instrument for my spite.

The first thing to grab my attention is a box of thumbtacks, all sharp and shiny. The second is a tube of powdered graphite, the kind of dry lubricant you use on locks. I point the end of the tube into the palm of my hand and squeeze out a charcoal-colored cloud.

"What the hell are you doing, Lucien?" Maxwell asks.

"Tit for tat," I reply, offering no further explanation.

The door to Mother's room creaks on its hinges as I open the door.

The Monet prints call me from across the room.

I look over her drug-addled, unconscious form and close my fist around a handful of thumbtacks. They pinch and pierce the soft flesh of my palm.

I stare at the Impressionist garbage and wonder how my father could have ever loved such a thing. I squeeze more graphite from the tube.

Mother is snoring, her mouth agape. I pour the tacks into her mouth, then pinch her nose shut. She gasps and swallows them. Panicked convulsions overtake her as the sharp tips bite at her tongue and paint red brushstrokes down her esophagus.

With the wild movements of a child fingerpainting, I smear the fine powder all across the Monet print, soiling the only thing Mother has left that bound her and Father together.

"Lucien?" Maxwell asks, his voice wavering.

"Monet was a shared passion between my

parents," I explain, before moving to the next print. "Tit for tat."

CHAPTER 4

It's the Wednesday after Labor Day, and Maxwell has convinced me to try out for the glee club. His argument? That it would get us out of a few study halls and that bad music was better than no music. I think his greater motivation is the delusion that his exceptional voice might overshadow his exceptional weight and loosen the pants of some less than exceptional glee club girl.

Of course, I have no genuine intention of joining. Lucien Beaumont singing teen pop covers? No. Posterity would hardly forgive that. I'm here for Maxwell's sake and, I must admit, out of morbid curiosity.

Mrs. Resnick, a social studies teacher who coaches the glee club, is calling students to the stage. An athletic kid in a Junior Varsity jacket approaches the mic. He has a goofy excitement to him, mixed with confidence of such a degree that it betrays a lack of self-awareness.

He snaps his fingers four times and begins singing some radio song I've never heard. His notes are inconsistent, and irony drips from his cocksure smile as he sings about being a princess. Each bar is met with a twist of his hips and a shake of his head. His lack of talent goes unnoticed by most of the students in the auditorium, who are more easily amused by idiot theatrics than singing.

Mrs. Resnick makes a comment about how great his energy will be for the club. I squint, not quite believing what I've just heard.

"Did she just say he made it in?"

"Everyone makes it," Maxwell whispers. "It's hyper-inclusive, so it's full of shitty singers who will make us look even better."

"If they don't turn anyone away, then why in the hell have tryouts?"

"I guess it's more to gauge where everyone is at."

A huff pushes past my lips as I lean back in the chair. I should have expected that the lack of standards at this school should extend beyond academics and into the arts. Already bored, I pull a marker from my bag and start drawing on the seat in front of me to pass the time. A cartoon of the Nutcracker's Rat King, complete with sword and crown, takes shape on the vinyl upholstery. As crude as my drawing is, it is infinitely more inspired than anything else masquerading as art in this auditorium.

It's 2:06, and a doughy girl with kinky hair is butchering a Disney tune.

It's 2:10, and a flamboyantly gay teen is muddling through Elton John's *Your Song*.

It's 2:25, and a girl with olive skin and television good looks closes her eyes in front of the microphone. Her voice is soft but confident as she sings the opening words to a radio ballad I'm vaguely familiar with. With each line she builds power, and each note is true and clear. As she approaches the chorus and leaves the narrow range of the verse behind she becomes a powerhouse. Mrs. Resnick and all the students, Maxwell included, are cheering and clapping for her, even before she finishes.

"Who is that?" I ask, enraptured.

"Violet Sarkissian," Maxwell answers. "The most popular girl in the senior class."

I watch her burgundy lips part with each note and her chest push out with each breath. My lungs are crushed in a vice. I'm angry and moved and feverish all at once. Without a word I rise and fumble my way along the seats toward the middle aisle of the auditorium. Maxwell calls after me, asking where I'm going, but I don't have the breath to answer.

No eyes stray from Violet as she nails the finale of her song. No one but Maxwell gives thought to my exit. What am I to them, in light of her?

Violet's stops singing, and there is more applause. I don't look back. Instead, I place my hand on the auditorium door, eager for the fresh air beyond.

"Where you going, new kid?" a feminine voice calls out over the microphone. "I heard you were some kind of musical prodigy."

I pause for a moment, then open the door without turning back.

"I wouldn't want to go on after me either," she says as if joking, even though she's not.

My hand slips away from the door, and I turn back. She's smiling at me, but there's malice in it. She means to challenge me so that she might brag that the son of Louis Beaumont was afraid to go against her.

Craning my neck to either side, I adjust my Windsor knot and walk to the stage. The other students howl like baboons, eager to escalate the tension. A few call out insults. I ignore them and ascend the steps to the stage.

My TV pretty nemesis steps aside with a measured grace. Her smirk is shiny with cherry lip gloss and venom. I approach the microphone and look out at the gathered students. Some are laughing and making fun. Others sit in silence, unsure what to expect. Maxwell gives me two goofy thumbs up from his seat.

"You gonna sing, big shot?" Violet whispers.

I had not planned on singing, and even as I part my lips part I know not what words or melody will issue forth until they hit my ears.

"Freude, schöner Götterfunken, Tochter aus Elysium,"

Maxwell lets out a howl of approval followed by a bellow of "Ludwig van!"

"Wir betreten feuertrunken, Himmlische, dein Heiligtum!"

My voice booms through the auditorium, hammering the simple but powerful melody of Beethoven's Ninth. The lyrics I sing are from the Schiller's *Ode to Joy,* in the original German as the composer intended. The Anglicized version, *Joyful, Joyful, We Adore Thee,* is another poem entirely, and it lacks the fire and majesty of Schiller's words. I'm sure the lukewarm souls that make up the student body of Swift River High would be infinitely more comfortable with the English version, but I don't sing this for them. I sing it in defiance of them.

"Deine Zauber binden wieder"

In defiance of their disposable, pop songs.

"Was die Mode streng geteilt;"

In defiance of their rudderless, *laissez-faire* worldviews.

"Alle Menschen werden Brüder,"

In defiance of their veneer of acceptance and inclusion.

"Wo dein sanfter Flügel weilt."

My voice batters their dullard ears.

Maxwell is on his feet cheering. Two other students join him—dangerous-looking kids dressed in the black-on-black uniform of some subculture or another. Mrs. Resnick is applauding with gusto. I turn toward the talented if uncultured Violet Sarkissian and return her smirk. She purses her lips but nods in reluctant approval.

"That was amazing," Mrs. Resnick says. I try to fight against the smile that is curling upward.

"It was adequate," Violet adds.

"That was what? Mozart?" Mrs. Resnick asks.

Maxwell's face goes powder white. Mine, if the heat in my cheeks is any indication, turns volcanic red.

"Mozart?" I ask, not bothering to hold back my astonishment and disgust. "Mozart?"

"Not Mozart? I'm more of a show tune gal," she says with a carefree laugh.

"That was *Ode to Joy,* by Ludwig van Beethoven. Perhaps the greatest gift Western civilization has ever received."

Mrs. Resnick playfully bumps the palm of her hand against her forehead.

"Silly me," she says with a laugh. "I should have known that."

I shift my gaze around the room, from one face to the next. Mrs. Resnick and her lack of consideration about her own ignorance. Violet Sarkissian, her talent and beauty wasted glorifying garbage music. The half dozen crap singers who came to have fun instead of pursuing art.

"I . . ."

Maxwell is looking at me, pleading wordlessly for me to tough it out and give this shitshow a chance.

"I apologize. I can't be party to this."

Mocking barbs erupt from the students as I leave the stage. They make fun of my choice of words and my choice of song. They shout insults about my clothes as if their ragged T-shirts and zipper hoodies are superior to my tailored shirt and tie. I ignore them, keeping my eyes on the exit door.

Ms. Kane offers me a Hershey's Kiss. I take it with a mumble of thanks, wishing to be anywhere else. The administration of Swift River High is concerned about my adjustment to life in a public school without the support I had at the Academy. As such, by edict of the school board, I'm to meet with the counselor weekly.

"Well, this is your time, Lucien," she says prodding me to open up. "What would you like to talk about?"

I stare at the foil-wrapped candy in my hand, enjoying the way it reflects the light.

"How about Paganini?" I ask. "Did you know he'd saw most of the way through all but one of his strings so that they might break mid-concert, leaving him to complete the performance with only one string? It was very dramatic. Quite the crowd pleaser."

"That's very interesting, but I was thinking we could talk about something more personal."

She doesn't sigh, or huff, or show any sign of frustration, despite my smartass answer. She either has an excellent poker face or her buttons are hard to push.

I peel back the foil and place the Kiss on my tongue. It begins melting immediately. I savor the taste and the excuse to stay silent.

"I heard you gave quite the performance at glee club tryouts. Care to talk about why you stormed out?"

"Because it was lame and cringeworthy. They weren't even tryouts. Everyone gets to join, regardless of merit. Just because they showed up!"

Ms. Kane writes something down in her notebook, some judgment of my mental health or my character.

"This isn't Broadway, Lucien," She says, dismissing my concerns. "This is just high school, and people are trying to have some fun while exploring the arts."

"I thought this was a place of learning. What does this teach anyone, Ms. Kane? That we're all special little snowflakes, regardless of talent or ambition? Or that standards in the arts don't matter, because art is subjective?"

She scribbles down another note.

"You don't think art is subjective?"

Her question makes me angry. It's a trap and a paradox. She means to make an idiot of me. If I say no, then I'm a soulless theorist, incapable of true musical experience. If I say yes, then my admission elevates Kanye West to the level of Rachmaninoff.

I stare at the foil from the Kiss, considering my words.

"What isn't subjective these days?" I ask, deflecting her question.

"That bothers you," she says, somewhere between inquiry and statement.

"I find it unsettling—the ambiguity in our age, of every idea and ideal."

She offers a slight smile. It's meant to reassure me, but there is such condescension in it.

"Well, perhaps we should find you another extracurricular that's less open to interpretation. Chess club, maybe? Or the mathletes?"

"That's okay," I tell her. "I have a part-time job and my own music. That's enough to keep me busy."

Her smile falters into an expression of disapproval. She recovers it quickly, but it's strained. She's not used to people telling her no.

"Your grades are excellent, but colleges want to see more than that. You need to pad those résumés with clubs and volunteer experience."

There's a passion in Ms. Kane's eyes as she speaks. She feels strongly about higher education. It is, to her, not something subjective like music or art, but objectively important.

"College isn't in the plan," I say, tossing the balled-up Kiss wrapper into her trash bin.

Her paid-for, prostitute-for smile goes flat. Disbelief is written across her face. I take joy at the crack in her façade.

"Why pay some bureaucracy the cost of a fine house, so they can force me into taking worthless electives and subjects that have no bearing on my career goals?"

Ms. Kane looks aghast at my words. I do my best not to crack a smile.

"And to bear that gross waste of time and money just so some blowhard academic can regurgitate musical theory at me? Or so that he might argue the case for anarchistic notions like atonality?"

She leans forward and shakes her head, no longer trying to hide her disapproval. My lips curl upward despite myself.

"Lucien, college is . . ."

"A hundred-thousand-dollar house party," I interrupt, "that comes with JStor and a meal plan."

Her mouth hangs open, but no words come out. I've stricken her silent. It's a small victory, but one that I needed today. It feels good, so I keep pushing.

"No. I'll leave this nightmare of a town behind and study under a working master. Maybe Javier Navarrete or one of my father's friends like

Philip Gravetree."

"Surely they wouldn't take you on without a degree. That's just not how the world works, Lucien. Even talent and nepotism only go so far."

"What is a piece of paper in this age of subjectivity and spectrum, Ms. Kane? Nothing is binary. There is no true or false or black or white. Nothing is set in stone. So what are professional expectations in this brave new world but another shackle to cast off?"

The record store is empty, save for myself. Jonas left to get a coffee an hour ago and hasn't come back. This happens a lot. I suspect that he gets talking about the good ole days with some other baby boomer at the coffee shop. The man can go on for hours about the civil rights movement, Woodstock, Simon and Garfunkel, and the benefits of marijuana.

I suppose we are alike in that way— both men out of time. Jonas yearns for the 1960s and I for the 1860s. His soul calls out for the world of his youth—an age of utopian dreams and anarchic revolution. I yearn for a world of order, like what came before his generation of self-important man-children unleashed chaos and disease upon every aspect of culture.

I don't mean for it to sound as if I dislike Jonas. That isn't the case at all. I find him more palatable than most adults. Most people really. He's very kind, thoughtful, and polite. We disagree a lot about music, but his arguments are well thought out and crafted with care. He just has an unrefined taste.

I'm happy to be alone in the store. It gives me time to muse over my father and Gravetree's ruined score. I copy what I can into my own songbook. Most of it is unreadable, but it's written on standardized staves, so I can tell how many bars are in each movement. I jot down the time signatures. The opening section, *Goetic Prelude in A minor,* is a 2/4 march. A standard 4/4 for the first movement, entitled *Black Unicorn Sonata.* The second movement, the title of which has been lost beneath black ink, is a waltz in 3/4.

I scan the visible notes. They play in my mind, forming a choppy dismembered tune, like brief moments of clear audio in a static-addled radio broadcast. I copy them onto my own staves, hungry for the lost sounds between each.

The bell over the door rings. It's a real, physical bell, not an electronic chime. For some reason that makes me happy.

Two kids from school walk in, dressed in all black. They're the ones who applauded my performance at the glee club tryouts. I'm not sure if they're goths or punks or metalheads. I never paid much attention to the distinctions between such things.

"Hey!" says one of them. "I thought you worked here."

He's tall, over six feet, and sickly thin. His hair is a long mane of black with the sides shaved down into something akin to a mohawk. His shirt bears an unreadable logo that looks like a tangle of thorns.

"That was sick, the way you fucking killed it with the Ninth and then just walked out of the auditorium, man."

"Thank you," I say, waiting for some punchline or sarcasm.

"I was gonna get up there and belt out some Fat Bottom Girls," adds the other boy, who's dressed in a button-up, with stretch jeans, all matching the midnight tone of his spiked black hair and sunglasses. "But I figured I'd get suspended for triggering one of those bulimic bitches."

The kid with the long mohawk lets out a brief laugh. I fake a smile, trying to be polite.

"I'm Asher," the tall kid with the long mohawk says, extending his hand toward me.

"Lucien," I say, shaking his hand. His grip is surprisingly firm, suggesting a strength greater than one might expect from his slender form and discipline that seems surprising given his appearance.

The other boy, the one with the spiked hair and sunglasses, introduces himself as J. C. His handshake isn't as firm as Asher's, and there is an awkward stiffness to it as if he's overthinking the form behind the movement.

There's a moment of silence. Asher picks up a CD from the dollar bin on the counter while J. C. shuffles back and forth with his hands in his pockets. I sit behind the counter, rocking my pen between two fingers. I'm still not sure why these boys are here. Did they come to commiserate about the embarrassment of a mutual enemy? Are they just buying music?

"It's a shame that glee club is the entirety of the music program," I finally say, breaking the quiet.

"Who needs some gay ass school program?" Asher asks, scanning through the tracklist on the back of a CD from the counter. "We could start our own thing, and it would be a hundred times cooler."

He pulls his gaze off the CD and looks at me.

"Our own thing?" I ask. "I'm not really a rock band kind of guy."

"Rock's dead," Asher replies. "Punks think drinking Pabst Blue Ribbon and voting Democrat is a big fuck-you to the system. Metal's been taken over by party-time scenesters and pearl-clutching humanists."

"It's all been castrated," J. C. adds, grabbing his crotch, then tearing his hand away. "No balls!"

The CD I have on the stereo comes to an end. I walk over and replace it with Bach's *Mass in B minor.*

"So what are you suggesting, gentlemen?"

"We do something like this," Asher says, pointing toward the speakers from which the Monteverdi Choir masterfully sings Bach's greatest work. "A real proper choir, not this glee club bullshit."

I'm taken aback. Neither Asher or J. C. strike me as choral singers. I might buy them having a passing interest in classical music, as I know many genres draw from the Western masters, but to this extent? The thought still lingers that this might be a joke at my expense.

"If you guys just came in here to fuck with me, could we get to the punchline? I was in the middle of something."

"No joke, man," Asher says with his hands raised defensively. "What you did today was punk as fuck, taking it to those pop retards with some real old-school shit."

"Between the three of us maybe we can bring some actual music to this hole in the ground," J. C. says.

Are they being sincere, I wonder. My gaze bounces back and forth between them. They look expectant, hanging on my words for an answer. Perhaps, I think, they're for real.

I glance down at the score my father and Gravetree wrote. Most of it is lost, but I do know it's a madrigal, written for a countertenor, two tenors, and a baritone.

"Between the four of us," I mumble. "Our choir would need four voices."

CHAPTER 5

I'm twelve years old again. Mother hasn't come home for days, and I'm too worried to do more than pick at my breakfast. White, salty streaks decorate my cheeks like cheap face paint. Somewhere in my mind, I know this love for my mother to be a relic. This type of concern is a bygone thing, but it feels immediate.

Father and I get dressed. Even today, with all this going on, he takes the time to make sure our shirts are tucked just so and our ties are straight.

Fed and dressed, we get in the car. We're going to get Mother, he tells me. I'm unsure how he knows where she is. He knows just about everything, though, so it's no real surprise, and I'm glad he does.

We wind up at a run-down apartment building a few towns away. It's the neighborhood she grew up in. Most of her family still lives here, but we rarely visit. They don't get along with Father.

The front door of the building is propped open with a wet, rolled-up copy of the Sunday Globe, so we don't bother ringing the bell. The hallway beyond is lined with nondescript brown doors. Awful smells permeate the floors and the walls—cigarettes, *cat piss, and pungent food.*

We walk up a flight of stairs and stop outside of an apartment. A tarnished number nailed to the door declares it unit number six, though there is the faded ghost of a seven on the wood beside it.

Father knocks. He's not gentle, and he is entirely unconcerned with waking up any of the neighbors. After his third try knocking, each series of rapping louder than the last, he tells me to back up. In a rare act of brutishness, he lifts his knee and boots the door. The frame breaks, and splinters rain around him.

The smell that comes from inside the apartment is worse than the stink of the hallway. It smells like burning plastic and rotten food. Father pushes past the door, which now hangs crooked in the frame. As we enter, he tells me to watch where I step.

Stray sunrays creep in around blankets tacked over the windows. It's a studio apartment, and the single room is littered with cans, bottles, and fast food packages. Mother lies on a mattress surrounded by trash. She's mostly undressed, her breasts exposed, and she lies next to a man I've never seen. A prescription bottle lay next to her, and blue pills have spilled out onto the mattress and into a puddle of wine on the floor. An end table sits next to the other side of the mattress, the side next to the stranger she's lying with. A bent spoon rests there, next to a syringe.

Father kneels beside Mother, red wine soaking into his gray slacks. He presses two fingers against her neck and places his ear by her mouth.

"She's okay, Lucien," he says, then corrects himself. "She'll be okay."

He pulls out his cellphone and dials 911 before telling me to wait in the hall. I stand there, afraid that if I take my eyes off of Mother she's going to die right then and there. Father yells this time, commanding me to wait in the hall. I burst into to tears and do as I'm told.

Inside my father is on the phone with an emergency dispatcher. He's asking for an ambulance. I poke my head in and watch from the hall. He doesn't see me.

He tells the dispatcher that his wife and another man have overdosed. His wife is alive, he says, but the man doesn't seem to be breathing. I can see the guy's chest rising and falling, even as my father says this.

He hangs up the phone and yanks the pocket square from his jacket. Using it as a tissue, he picks up the needle from the end table and pulls back the plunger.

"You can't have them," he mumbles, "but I'll give you him."

He jabs the needle into the man's arm and presses the plunger down. A second later he takes it out and places it back on the table. He then folds up the pocket square and puts it back in his breast pocket.

"I'll be right there, Lucien!" he shouts, without looking back to me.

Music starts playing from inside the apartment. It's dark, minor key stuff, and parts of it sound familiar. It takes me a few moments to *determine its source, then I realize that my father is humming. He pulls a tiny notebook and a pen from his pocket, then scribbles something down. His head bobs up and down in rhythm as he hums the same melodies over and over, skipping notes one time and finding them the next.*

Sirens wail out in the street, and Father abruptly rises.

The morning alarm from my phone awakens me. My dream has left me with the gift of song. The melody plays on repeat in my brain and I hum it, over and over, afraid that it will dissipate with the retreating haze of sleep. I stumble to my desk and draw a crooked, uneven stave, then fill in the notes that are playing in mind.

It isn't much, just a few bars. I feel as if I should know it—as if it is a thing that has existed in the real world and not just in my mind.

The vandalized score for *The Madrigal of the World's End* sits on my desk. I open it to the first page and compare the notes unscathed by my mother's anger from the first few measures with my own dream-born scribbles. They match. The first quarter note from the opening bar of the treble clef is a middle C on both. A double eighth note from B to E appears on the third bar of both their bass clef and mine. So on and so on.

It's Thursday morning, and I won't be going to school today. I'm on to something with the score—a reversal of Mother's savage disfigurement of the Beaumont legacy. I rush out to my piano with the ruined score and my own scribbled notes. I prop them up on the music stand and begin to play the opening measures from *Goetic Prelude in A minor*.

A soothing and powerful coolness flows from the keys and into my body. The air vibrates, not just with the cry of piano strings, but with an otherworldly ambiance—a dissonant sound beyond the range of human hearing that rattles my being.

The music is regal and melancholy. The song of dispossessed kings and fallen angels. The song of dead patriarchs and ghosts from nobler ages.

In less than a minute I reach the end of my sloppy sheet music. The last note resonates, unresolved, like the slow hiss of a dying man's final word. I run my middle finger along the blacked-out lines of Father's score as if my touch alone might reveal what else lies beneath.

I play the selection from my dream again, then once more. With a firm grip on the melody, I try to speculate what might come next, based on the stray notes I can make out from the score, my familiarity with Father's style, and my own musical intuition. I tap out variations of the theme across the keys, replacing notes from earlier bars with their octaves or fifths. I try endless combinations of notes within A minor, then move out of scale into the realm of the atonal.

Nothing sounds right.

Nothing feels right.

Nothing possesses the magic of those first few measures.

Minutes at the piano become hours. The

morning fades away like memories of the dead, and I am no closer to figuring out this lost song than I was at dawn.

It's Thursday, just past noon, and Mother's bedroom door screeches on its hinges. I hear her stumble out behind me, but I don't bother to turn. She asks if I should be at school. I tell her it's the weekend, and she doesn't challenge my lie.

Her footfalls are uneven on the floor, messing up my meter and rhythm. *I pick the pen up from my songbook and grip it tight.* The sound of her steps softens as she crosses into the kitchen. The refrigerator opens with a hiss. Tupperware thumps against plastic bottles. *Ink drips from the ballpoint tip like venom from a scorpion's tail.* Mother comes back through the living room, sloshing around a drink as she stumbles back to bed. *The piano bench topples as I spin around and loose my pen like a dart. It finds its mark in Mother's carotid artery. She falls to her knees. The ebony ink pumps into her bloodstream, blackening the veins beneath her skin, like the wild brushstrokes she painted across Father and Gravetree's score.*

Mother's door closes without a word. My pen is broken in my hand, and black ink stains my palm. I walk over to the rubbish barrel in the kitchen and drop it in.

A paper shopping bag filled with recycling sits on the floor beside the trash. It occurs to me as I look down at the discarded menus and torn envelopes in the recycling that Gravetree might have his own copy of *The Madrigal*.

I dump the bag out on the kitchen table,

searching through junk mail and cardboard. I toss aside dry nips and empty pill bottles until I find the envelope that our symphony tickets came in.

I'm in luck. The return address is Gravetree's home, rather than a P.O. box or an office. It's only in Cambridge. Depending on the train schedule, I can be there in two hours.

It doesn't take long for me to gather my things—my own songbook, along with the scrap of music I jotted down this morning, the score for *The Madrigal,* and the envelope with Gravetree's address. With them secure in my backpack I lay out my best suit and adjourn to the shower.

I exit the Harvard Square train station on JFK Street, surrounded by a mixed crowd of academics, professionals, and layabouts. It's a strange sort of nexus point, this place. A man in front of me, dressed in a suit much finer than my own, shouts into his phone about missing a birthday over a business meeting and how he'll make it up. Across the street, a group of white Harvard students who look like Abercrombie models hold up signs calling for an end to their own privilege. Homeless punk rockers idle the day away, blasting music about change and revolution while heckling passers-by for beer money.

Looking around, I wonder how mankind has gotten this far. The many tiny spirits riding upon the shoulders of history's few giants, I suppose.

Gravetree lives on Auseil Way, just a few blocks outside of the square. The street is an incredibly long and narrow one-way, past the Harvard commons where nannies take other people's children to play but before the hip little boutiques and restaurants that line Mass Ave.

His house is a three-level Victorian that appears to have fallen into disarray long ago. Blisters and curls of washed-out paint cling to the exterior. The color varies between deep burgundy and grayish pink. A set of tarnished numbers nailed to the door declare it number 67. It isn't as big as what we had on Raylene Street, and much worse for wear, but considering its location the house probably cost him three times as much.

I ascend a small wooden staircase to the front door. A brass plaque beside the doorbell reads *Gravetree,* assuring me that I have the right address. I press the cracked plastic button and a two-note chime plays within.

A small window is set head height within the door, held in place by dried, cracking glazing. I try to peer in, but filth coats the glass, preventing me from seeing if Gravetree is coming or not. No sound comes from behind the door, and after a minute I ring again.

"Hold your water!" a voice calls out.

Footsteps and groaning follow the cry. After half a minute or so I hear a deadbolt click, and the door opens a few inches. Gravetree looks out through the crack, the links of a chain lock pulled taught between us.

"Mr. Gravetree," is all I'm able to say before he cuts me off.

"I don't need Jesus, and I don't vote!" he grumbles and goes to close the door. I push back with my foot, not allowing him to dismiss me.

"Mr. Gravetree, my name is Lucien Beaumont."

"You're Louis's son," he mutters with an expression somewhere between acknowledgment and terror.

I nod and pull my foot back from the door. He slams it shut, fumbles with the chain, then opens it all the way.

"Come in, come in," he beckons.

The inside of the house is not as I expected, appearing to be in worse condition than the exterior. The foyer is dark and musty, the smells of mold and cherry tobacco fighting for dominance. To the left of the doorway piles of mail overflow from an ancient end table. A greasy chandelier hangs from the ceiling, mottled with brown spots.

Gravetree himself is not as I expected either. He's a feeble, trembling old man, a far cry from the impassioned conductor I witnessed at the symphony or the lively musician I remember seeing share a bottle with my father on so many nights. Up this close, I can see that one of his eyes is glazed white with cataracts. A silver five o'clock shadow covers his sunken cheeks and pointed chin. He's barefoot, dressed in a stained WGBH T-shirt and a pair of denim shorts that expose an unwholesome amount of flesh.

He shakes my hand, the tremors in his body stronger than his grip. His skin is fever hot and coarse with eczema.

"I should have known right away. You look so much like your dad," he says, amazement written on his face. "Your father and I used to discuss the idea of immortality through art, but this"—grasping my shoulder in a weak hand—"this is immortality! Flesh and bone!"

"I hope I'm not intruding, sir," I reply, not knowing what else to say.

"Nonsense! Come have a seat."

Gravetree leads me away from the foyer, down a dim hallway decorated in hundred-year-old linen wallpaper. Gilded deer and black unicorns are frozen in an eternal frolic against a field of jade linen.

The walls are lined with portraits of what I must assume are Gravetree's favorite composers. The portraits are not uniform in size, nor do the frames match. Some are plain, light wood, others carved ornately and stained dark. Not even the style or medium is consistent from one portrait to the next. Bach is rendered in richly textured oil. Liszt is painted in watercolors. Samuel Barber's portrait isn't even a painting but rather a black-and-white photograph.

"Is this your pantheon of gods?" I ask.

He laughs at this.

"I call it my hall of heroes, but it's far from complete. Just a few pieces I've acquired here and there."

We pass an open door on the right that leads to a cluttered parlor with a baby grand sitting in one corner. Pages of sheet music are strewn across the piano's top, and a dozen or so scores are stacked on the floor beside it. The sweet smell of cherry tobacco wafts out from the doorway.

Gravetree leads me to the end of the hall and

into the kitchen. Like all the other rooms, it is dimly lit. Little daylight makes it through the windows given how tightly the houses on the street are packed together.

"Tea?" he asks, ushering me toward a heavy, wooden table. "Or I have some Moxie."

"Tea would be wonderful."

I sit down and place my backpack on the floor, noting the cracking linoleum. Gravetree fills an ancient kettle and puts it on the stove, giving me a chance to take in the kitchen. The ceiling is sagging with water damage, and grease coats the windows. Old, peeling wallpaper decorates the kitchen, just as it had the hallway. Here it is full-color still-lifes— overflowing cornucopias and arrangements of vibrant fruit set against a field of tobacco-stain yellow that may have once been white.

"I wanted to thank you for the symphony tickets."

"Oh, it was my pleasure, Lucien. Your father was a great admirer of Gorecki, so I thought you might be as well."

"He's one of my favorites, sir. And it was an excellent performance."

Gravetree fumbles through a cabinet, pulling out several boxes of tea. He calls out each flavor like an individual question. "Earl Grey? French Vanilla? Egyptian Licorice?"

"French Vanilla, please."

A shrill whistle issues from the kettle. Gravetree retrieves two mugs from his cabinet, and I wonder about their cleanliness, though I keep my concerns to myself. He prepares a cup for each of us and joins me at the kitchen table.

"So what brings you here, young master Beaumont?"

There is a nervousness to him but also an expression of genuine happiness. It's an odd juxtaposition, and I wonder if perhaps the old man is losing his mind just a little.

From my backpack I produce *The Madrigal of the World's End.* All color drains from Gravetree's complexion as I place it before him. His trembling becomes a full-on fit of palsies. Steaming tea overflows from his cup. It must be burning his hand, but he doesn't pay any mind to the pain, seemingly hypnotized by the sight of the score he helped compose.

"The Madrigal," he breathes, almost a whisper.

"I knew you and Father had collaborated, so I went through his notes after your performance this weekend."

He stares at me, tears pooling in his wild eyes. I decide at this moment that there is something wrong with Philip Gravetree. The filthy house, the poor hygiene, the nervous trembling—these, it seems, are not quirks or eccentricities, but the symptoms of insanity or dementia.

"He had this? This was in your home?"

"Yes," I say, keeping my tone as even as I can manage. "But someone has vandalized it. The pages aren't readable."

I open the songbook to show Gravetree the broad strokes of ink obscuring the staves. He turns his head and lets out some incomprehensible exclamation.

"I think I may have figured out a few bars this morning, but that's all I could manage to play."

"You played the song?" A vein is bulging on his forehead as he yells the question.

"I . . . I think so, but the score is so damaged I'm only speculating. I was hoping you might help me fill in the blanks."

Gravetree snatches the score from the table. He paces the kitchen, flipping through it, muttering and shaking his head.

"How did you play it?" There is a severity to his tone, accompanied by a fierce and sudden sense of lucidity. "There isn't enough left unmarred here to make heads or tails."

"I . . . I think I heard it in my dream last night."

He runs a hand through his unkempt white hair and tears begin to roll down his cheeks. His visceral reaction to *The Madrigal* is leaving me increasingly uneasy. I fight the urge to excuse myself and leave, quite sure that Gravetree is my only chance at procuring an undamaged copy of his and Father's score.

"Why, Louis?" He screams the question at the heavens, his arms raised in dramatic fashion. "Why would you keep this in your home?"

I push back in my chair, careful not to move too suddenly. Gravetree is clearly unstable, and I fear he might be easily spooked into violence.

"Mr. Gravetree, I'm sorry to have upset you. I only thought you might help me fill in the blanks."

"Oh, I'll help you, Lucien."

Gravetree turns a knob on the stove, and after a few clicks an orange flame comes to life. He touches one corner of the score to the flame, and my heart catches in my throat. The paper blackens and curls as fire dances up its surface.

"I'll do what your father should have."

Now I'm the one with tears welling in my eyes. I shoot up from my chair, sending it tumbling to the floor.

"That's my father's," my voice trembles with anger.

Gravetree drops the burning score onto the open flame. In just a few instants *The Madrigal* burns away before my eyes.

In the flames I see the head of a unicorn, born from smoke and ash. The creature shakes out its black mane, casting embers into the air.

My hands tighten into fists, and the only thing keeping me from attacking Gravetree is the fact that I've already copied the ruined score.

A choir, rendered in orange flame, joins the magnificent beast in the fire of the gas range. They sing the song from my dream.

"That song is a curse!" he shouts, spittle flying from his lips.

I scowl and join the unicorn's choir in singing what little I know of the tenor part. Gravetree stumbles back in horror. He covers his ears and screams for me to stop. I refuse.

The few bars I have figured take only seconds to sing, but the unicorn does what Gravetree refused to. It begins to fill my mind with the lost notes, revealing more of the song. I keep singing as the beast in the fire conducts. The power pulsing through my body dwarfs what I felt at my piano in the morning.

"Get out!" Gravetree screams. "Get out of my house!"

The unicorn's voice fades and its smoky image dissolves, as the last bits of the score turn to ash. A single word resonates in my mind as the music stops.

Listen.

Gravetree rushes at me; he pushes me with all the might his feeble body can muster. I stand my ground, snorting in derision as he pounds a gnarled fist against my chest.

"Get the hell out of here with that song!"

I pick up my backpack and sling it over one shoulder. I thank him for the tea and show myself out. He follows, bellowing about curses and devils dancing upon eighth notes.

I open the door and step out of Philip Gravetree's wretched home, back into the fresh September air. As I cross the threshold he calls my name. He sounds lucid again. I turn to face him.

"Forget *The Madrigal,* Lucien. For your own sake and everyone else's."

His expression is one of pleading. There is a desperation to him, which adds an extra, pitiable dimension to his slovenly, infirm demeanor.

Without another word he closes the door. I stand there for a moment on the rickety steps of number 67 Auseil Way, processing what has just happened and how quickly things escalated. I straighten my tie and ponder Gravetree's insane reaction to the sight of his own composition. I consider the vision I saw in flames as the score burned and the music revealed to me by the unicorn.

The music. I need to write it down before the notes flee my mind.

I kneel down on Gravetree's stairs and retrieve my own songbook from my backpack. I fill in the bars taught to me in my vision by the choir of flame, and they match up with the notes I was able to copy from Father and Gravetree's score, as I knew they would.

From inside the house I hear a piano playing and Gravetree singing. The music is strange, played in an odd meter. Bars begin with strong resolve and decline in tension with each passing note. Accents fall on the second beat instead of the third.

The final words of the unicorn come to mind. Listen, it had said. So I do.

It's Thursday afternoon, and I sit on Gravetree's steps, my back against his front door, listening to him sing and play his mad song on his baby grand. Turning to a new section of the songbook, I transcribe what I hear as best as I'm able. It's impossible for my pen or my mind to keep up with his playing, but I manage to capture a passing, if inadequate, transcription of his manic performance.

CHAPTER 6

It's Friday morning, and I'm dodging red rubber balls in a fetid gymnasium. Maxwell is next to me, sweating and panting. Moist abstractions, saltwater Rorschach blots, soak through his plain white T-shirt. "Can you hang around after school today?" I ask him as a gust of wind kisses my cheek and I avoid being hit in the face.

"Sure. What's up?"

Someone launches another red ball my way. I manage to avoid it, but Maxwell isn't so lucky. The ball smacks against his forehead, and he falls on his generous behind. The gym breaks into a fit of laughter.

The P.E. teacher blows his whistle, calling a timeout. I offer Maxwell my hand and help him off the floor. Ari Cole, who stands in the opposing line, calls out a joke about us holding hands. More laughter.

"I'll tell you after class," I say before Maxwell shuffles off the court.

Physical education here at Swift River High is a crude thing, designed for the lowest common denominator. It makes me yearn for the Academy, where we would hike through the wilderness, compete in archery, and study fencing. But those days are gone.

The ball is returned to the opposing team, and Ari gets hold of it. He grins with stupid, blue-collar charm and flexes the muscles that come with being a second-time senior.

"Don't worry," he calls out at Maxwell, who's sitting down on the bleachers. "Your boyfriend's gonna be out in just a second."

I raise my middle finger and blow a kiss in Ari's direction. It drifts through the air and lands on his forehead. His skin blisters and smolders at its touch.

The gym teacher blows his whistle, signaling the game to resume. Ari feigns two throws before whipping the ball at me as hard as he can. I jump to the side. It hits another kid and bounces off his chest before landing at my feet. I scramble for the ball and hurl it toward Ari. He sidesteps it and sneers at me.

"That's how you want it, Beaumont?"

Another kid from the opposite team, someone whose name I don't know, has the ball. Ari rips it from his hand and tries his best to take my head off with it. The ball misses by a hair and slams into the wall with a vicious smack. Someone behind me picks it up and throws it back across the line, where they eliminate a scrawny kid with dreadlocks.

Ari rushes for the ball again. There's anger and meanness in his eyes as he hums the red orb straight at my face. I close my eyes and raise my hands. The rubber slaps against my palms, and the tender skin burns beneath its touch. That's okay though, because I don't drop the ball. Ari is out, and it's because of me.

"Oh, fuck you!" he screams.

"That's detention, Cole," the gym teacher shouts.

"Oh, for fucking what?" Ari asks, still steaming with anger.

"Language. Now go hit the showers."

I smile, watching Ari storm back to the locker room. It makes me so happy, in fact, that I almost enjoy the rest of the game.

There are only ten minutes left in gym class. They pass quickly. A whistle blows, calling the game and dismissing us all to the locker room. A few kids around me are grumbling about our side losing, but I could care less. I join Maxwell by the bleachers, and we make our way out back.

"So, what's up after school?" he asks.

"I met some other kids who want to sing. Real music, not that glee club garbage."

"For real?" he asks, a big dumb smile written across his face.

"We're meeting by the auditorium at three. It could be a waste of time, but maybe not."

We follow the procession of students into the locker room, which smells tenfold worse than the gymnasium itself. My sneakers smack against tile wet with god knows what. Maxwell asks me something, but his question is lost beneath the laughter and howls of two dozen seniors.

"Oh man, that's not even right," I hear someone say.

"Aww, shit!" another voice yells.

We push through to see what all the buzz is about. Everyone is circled around the center of the locker room, where my suit is laid out on the floor, covered in piss.

"Looks like someone had an accident," some kid I've never seen before shouts. His comment is met with a hail of laughter.

The fluorescent overhead lights burst, and sparks rain across the gathered students. An electrical fire erupts in the walls, and black smoke billows into the room. The acrid clouds take on the forms of demons and unicorns invading the mouths and noses of all save Maxwell and myself. It chokes them. It sears their lungs, their throats, their eyes. They fall where they stand, onto my piss-covered clothes, and I ask why they aren't laughing anymore. No one answers.

"Mr. Beaumont, shorts are only to be worn in gym class," Mr. Jackson says. My American literature classmates erupt into laughter. News of my piss-covered clothes has spread beyond the locker room, and a video is spreading throughout the student body of me trying to wash my suit in the showers.

"I'm sorry, Mr. Jackson, but some subhuman animal peed all over my clothes," I say in a matter of fact tone.

The students laugh again, but the teacher lets out a loud "Whoa!" Everyone quiets down, startled by the furious sneer on Mr. Jackson's face. For a moment I assume he is angry at these dregs for laughing at my misfortune, but I'm wrong.

"We don't use words like subhuman in my classroom, Mr. Beaumont. Words like that sent six million people into gas chambers. Words like that hung my ancestors from trees."

Confusion grips me for a few moments, then the feeling turns to anger as I realize I'm getting in trouble for Ari fucking Cole spraying his diseased piss all over my suit.

"Why don't you take a walk down to the office?"

I slam down my copy of *The Scarlet Letter,* a degenerate book that makes light of marriage and raises a cheating whore upon the pedestal of victimhood, and I glare at Mr. Jackson. He stares back, angry and unflinching.

"Someone literally urinated all over my clothes. They ruined a very expensive suit and a silk tie that cost more than your laptop. And you're concerned about what words I use to insult them?"

"Privileged white boys who can afford to wear suits every day don't get to use hate speech in my classroom."

The first bar from The Madrigal's *prelude plays over the intercom, scratchy and low-fi, but nonetheless powerful. Mr. Jackson's eyes explode into flame within his skull. His howls of agony accompany the song coming from the speakers, and the juxtaposition is not unpleasant.*

"Office."

Liquid flame drips down the teacher's face, leaving dead, dry carbon in place of flesh. The rest of his body combusts, the fire devouring him. His charred form collapses and crumbles into a pile of black ash.

"Now."

I pick up my backpack and leave the class. The halls are empty, and for that I'm thankful. There is a measure of peace to be found in solitude. It cools the anger in my heart.

On the way to the principal's office, I stop by the bathroom. I place my backpack on the sink and stare into a graffiti-covered mirror. I don't like what I see looking back at me. A bullied weakling, robbed of his clothes and dignity. A disgraced noble, with a besmirched family name, forced to walk as a pariah among the resentful common.

I choke back my tears and retrieve a flask—Father's flask—from my bag. The juniper smell of Bombay Sapphire drifts out as I twist the cap. I close my eyes and take a long swallow. A cool sensation flows through my body, dulling the pain.

"Did you bring enough for the whole class?" a voice calls out from behind me.

Startled, I turn and find J. C. coming out from one of the stalls. He smirks and reaches out for the flask.

"Wash your hands first, you animal," I say.

"Fair enough," he says with a laugh.

I take another sip as he washes up. He dries his hands, and I pass him the flask. The drink brings an unsure expression to his face while he considers the taste.

"What is this?"

"Gin," I reply.

"I dig it," he says, knocking back another swig.

He passes the flask back. I seal it and return it to the bag. Before I zipper it closed I grab a tin of Altoids, taking one for myself then offering one to J. C.

"You don't want to finish off that flask?" he asks.

"Not before we sing later. Plus, I'm on my way to the office for saying mean things about the asshole who ruined my clothes."

"Yeah, I heard about that," he says, shaking his head. "I have an extra set of clothes in my locker if you want to borrow them. It's not Armani, but it is a step up from gym clothes."

"Thank you! That would be incredible."

"You're welcome, man," he replies and motions for me to follow him. We leave the bathroom and venture back into the empty halls. I think to myself again how nice it is when no one else is in the halls. It's as if everyone is dead but us.

"Why do you have extra clothes in your locker?" I ask.

"Ari Cole. Tyler Pulleo. Whoever pissed all over your clothes. I've been dealing with these cocksuckers since grade school. You learn to plan ahead."

School is over for the day. While the student body rushes for the buses, the bike racks, and the parking lot, Maxwell and I head down an empty hallway to the auditorium. Glee Club doesn't meet on Friday, so the space should be ours.

"So who are these other kids who want to start a choir?"

"Remember those punk, goth, whatever kids that cheered me when I sang the Ninth last week?"

"J. C. Ramirez and Asher Blinko?" Maxwell asks incredulously. "Lucien, they're like . . . bad kids."

I point to the clothes I'm wearing, a black and red bowling shirt with three sixes embroidered over the breast, and a pair of faded black jeans.

"If it wasn't for J. C. I'd be wearing a piss-drenched suit or my gym clothes, so he's okay in my book. Just give them a chance."

Maxwell doesn't seem convinced, but he doesn't argue. He follows me through the door and into the auditorium. It's dark save for the stage lights. Asher sits at a piano to the side of the stage, playing some tune I don't recognize with surprising skill. He wears a thrift store blazer and a Texas tie that bisects the black heart on his white T-shirt. Even with jeans it actually doesn't look horrible. I don't normally appreciate the whole rock star aesthetic, but he pulls it off.

"Welcome, maestro," J. C. shouts from the stage, where he lies with his head hanging over the edge. "How was your talk with the principal?"

"You got sent to the principal?" Maxwell asks, the concern in his voice almost comedic.

"I got a warning. He told me to watch my mouth moving forward, and to think about wearing something that attracts less attention."

"What a dick!" Asher shouts, still playing the piano.

We approach the stage. Asher and J. C. come to greet us with some mix of hand slap and shake that I awkwardly try to match. Maxwell, usually comfortably aloof, is guarded and quiet. He's afraid of these boys.

I suggest we start things off by determining everyone's range. Maxwell and I have already established our upper and lower limits, myself being a tenor and Maxwell performing best as a countertenor but capable of singing down to baritone. Asher tells me that he is more comfortable singing low and cites a few vocalists from beyond my own musical spheres—Peter Steele, Glenn Danzig, Johnny Cash. Maxwell tells me that all three of them are baritones. I play an A2, and Asher matches it. We work our way higher, note by note, until he fails. It turns out that Asher is indeed a classic baritone.

We find that J. C. has a tenor voice, with a range similar to my own. His singing has a rock 'n' roll coarseness to it that I don't care for, but he hits the notes.

It surprises me to find that both of them can read music. Asher took piano and drum lessons growing up, and J. C.'s parents forced him into flamenco guitar at a young age. There's more talent between them than I suspected.

"So you guys really like choral music?" Maxwell asks.

"Some. Darker shit like Barber and Tchaikovsky," J. C. says.

"Modern music is a study in castration, even in the underground," Asher says, reiterating his sentiment from the other day. "For all the posturing in punk and metal, there's nothing fucking rebellious or iconoclastic going on. But dudes like Wagner and Gesualdo—there's a timeless kind of danger to them."

I'm impressed for the second time today. Carlo Gesualdo, while an enormous talent, is no household name. It wouldn't surprise me if Asher knows him only for his crimes and excesses— murder, perversion, and masochism—but he does know him.

"Well, let's start with something simple but dark." I pull out several copies of the sheet music for *O Magnum Mysterium* by Tomas Luis de Victoria. It's a simple, minor-scale madrigal for four singers. Perfect for my little choir.

We spend the next forty minutes familiarizing everyone with the piece. First, we listen to a recording of the Cambridge Singers performing it, then we review the sheet music part by part and bar by bar. Finally, we try it all together. I start things off, singing the first few measures alone. Maxwell joins in next with a higher part. Just before the eighth bar, I signal J. C. He hits the timing and pitch with precision. Eight beats later Asher's rich baritone joins us, swelling beneath our voices.

It sounds great for about one minute, then our timing falls apart. And that's fine. We have a proof of concept that this choir might actually work.

Asher brings up a metronome app on his phone and matches the tempo up to the recording of the piece. We begin again and make it twice as far. Maxwell's nervousness has subsided, and his natural good humor is shining through. He becomes increasingly comfortable with J. C. and Asher each time we try to get through the piece. I find myself less guarded as well. I smile and laugh between takes, far easier than I have in a very long time.

We get to our sixth run through of *O Magnum Mysterium,* and we nearly complete the short piece without a hitch, but then the auditorium doors open. Violet Sarkissian is standing in the entryway, the curves of her body exaggerated and accentuated by the interplay of light and shadow. Behind her are some of her glee club flunkies. I don't know their names, but I've created handles for them in my mind. The flamboyantly gay boy I call Fashion Queer. The jock with the J.V. jacket is Karaoke Joe. And then there's the girl with the kinky hair who likes to butcher Disney songs. I don't even bother making a name up for her, she's so far beneath my notice.

"Well, what do we have here?" Violet asks, walking toward us with the grace of a runway model.

"Hi, Violet," Maxwell says with a goofy smile. She glances at him with disdain.

"Did you freaks start your own glee club because you couldn't be around normal people and normal music?"

"This is not a glee club," I respond. "It's a proper choir."

They laugh at this. They laugh, and my blood boils.

"That explains the church music they were singing," Karaoke Joe says. "I thought they were just playing a game of priest and choir boys."

Another burst of laughter. My hands clench into fists.

Violet ascends the stairs to the stage and stares straight into my eyes. Her gaze is beautiful and disarming. It fills me with lust and wonder and rage.

"I don't think you have permission to be here." She's talking specifically to me. Venom drips from every word.

"It's a free country," J. C. chimes in.

"But school regulations dictate that a faculty member must be present for any club or extracurricular. No unsupervised students."

"Big surprise," Asher says, "bitch is a snitch."

"Watch your fucking mouth, freakshow!" Karaoke Joe yells.

Asher steps forward in the jock singer's direction. Maxwell takes a step back. The rest of us, on both sides, fall silent, waiting to see if things escalate.

Asher pulls a knife from his pocket and flips it open.

"You wanna do this, fuckface?"

Karaoke Joe goes still. No one says anything for a moment, then Fashion Queer puts a hand against his friend's chest and ushers him backward.

"Come on. It's not worth it," Fashion Queer says. "Let these psychos have their little black heart boys' choir."

"Let's go, Violet," the fat girl says.

Violet alone seems undeterred by Asher's blade. How nice it must be to have such confidence that nothing can go wrong that you have the guts to ignore a knife. What a charmed life she must have led so far to know no fear.

"Shame about your suit," she says with a big, fake smile that shows off her perfect teeth.

"This is nice too, though. This more"—she pauses and straightens my collar as she searches for the perfect words to devastate me—"pedestrian look is actually much more you."

Violet spins on her heel, turning her back to me. Her movements are almost dance-like.

I grab her by the hair and pull her back. Her sense of grace vanishes as her feet go out from beneath her, and she crashes to the stage.

She follows her friends down the dark aisle of the auditorium and toward the door, and I can't avert my gaze.

I bury my brogue into her stomach. Pain overtakes her, but even suffering looks sensual when written across her full lips.

Karaoke Joe raises one hand high above his head and flips us off without turning around.

Instead of moans or screams escaping Violet's mouth with each kick I deliver, she sings another bar from The Madrigal of the World's End. *Her voice is even more beautiful than her pain-addled face.*

The door slams behind the glee club. It echoes through the auditorium, the only sound for several seconds. J. C. shatters the quiet with a loud belch, eliciting laughter from Maxwell and Asher. I'm still focused on Violet and watching her sensual agony unfold in my mind.

"Black Heart Boys' Choir," Asher says. "I like it."

CHAPTER 7

I've stopped going to gym class. I should be there right now, or rather I'm scheduled to be there. The library, however, is a better fit. It's quiet here, and I find the presence and smell of books comforting.

Mrs. O'Donnell, the librarian, never bothers me or asks for a hall pass. She simply smiles and compliments my clothes as I pass by the desk. I shoot her a smile in turn before I sit down at a table tucked in the corner.

Maxwell is undoubtedly getting twice the abuse during gym because of my absence. That's his choice, though. I invited him to skip with me so that we might enjoy the quiet of the library together, but he declined. Poor Maxwell, so afraid of getting into trouble.

So here I sit alone with the patchwork songbook for *The Madrigal of the World's End*. The parts of the song revealed to me in dreams and visions line up with what was in Father's score. What I transcribed of Gravetree's playing, on the other hand, doesn't seem to work with Father's notes.

With my headphones plugged into my tablet,

I start tapping away at the digital keys of a free piano app. Gravetree's music, what I managed to commit to paper, is unconventional. Its rhythm is disjointed and its harmony erratic, almost as if . . .

"He's playing backward," I say aloud.

I skip to the last page I had transcribed while sitting outside of Gravetree's door, and I play it in reverse order on the piano app. For the first time it sounds like real music, and while it doesn't match up to my father's notes in melody or meter, there are certain leitmotifs undeniably shared between the two. What I have must be from a later movement, something from the pages that had been torn out of Father's score.

I'm missing notes here and there, having failed at keeping up with the old man's driven performance, and some of what I do have sounds off. My pen surely made mistakes as I hastily copied the melody into my songbook, but I have a good chunk of an entire movement, perhaps.

But why would Gravetree play it backward? I know that something about the piece spooked him, but is his mind so deteriorated that he must resort to such an absurd ritual to put himself at ease?

For the next forty minutes, while poor Maxwell suffers the ire of our idiot classmates in the gymnasium, I experiment with the piece. I make guesses to fill in the blanks, jotting down possibilities in red pen and swapping bad notes with others, hoping something will sound right.

The bell rings announcing the end of the period. I'm closer to revealing the song, but there are still holes, filled only with speculation and theory.

It's not good enough.

I gather my things and smile at Mrs. O'Donnell as I leave the library. Instead of taking a right toward my calculus class I head left and to the side exit by the eastern stairwell.

It's quarter past ten in the morning, and I'm going to visit Phillip Gravetree again.

There is no answer when I knock on the door of 67 Auseil Way. Not the first time. Not the second or third.

Staring in the tiny window on the door, I can see nothing beyond the filth that coats it. Not a shifting of light. Not an amorphous shadow. No sign of life.

I place my ear against the door, listening for the sound of a television or music being played. I'm met with silence.

The door is locked, but the old, tarnished knob wiggles in my grip. I give it a shove, hoping the door or the frame will give way, but neither does. It occurs to me that I could kick it in with little trouble, but that would call unwanted attention my way. Instead, I grab my laminated school ID and shove it into the space between the frame and the door. I've never tried to bypass a lock before, but I've seen this trick used in television and films. I'm astonished at how easy it really is. A few adjustments to the angle and a little bit of force, and voilà!

The door opens, and my senses need a moment to adjust. Every curtain in Gravetree's home is drawn, and the darkness inside stands in stark contrast to the sunlight bleeding in through the entryway. The dreariness is one thing, but the smell is another—even worse than I remember from my last visit. It's as if Gravetree's paranoia has taken on a putrid, physical form and mated with the invisible spores living in the damp carpeting, all the while dancing with the acrid smell of smoke and ash.

"Mr. Gravetree?" I call out, closing the front door behind me.

"Are you home, Mr. Gravetree? It's Lucien Beaumont."

No answer.

I walk down the hallway, his hall of heroes as he called it, and I nod in respect to a portrait of J. S. Bach before taking a right into the parlor. The place is still a mess, littered in sheet music, just as it had been last week. Papers are strewn across the top of the piano, and they cover the floor like dead leaves in a forest. Somewhere in there the crazy bastard must have a copy of the work he and Father composed together.

It smells like smoke in the parlor. Not like tobacco but something more wholesome, like a campfire.

On the music stand of Gravetree's piano sits a ruined spiral-bound songbook. All the pages are missing, leaving nothing but the cardboard covers. I lift up the gutted book and read the front. A unicorn's head is inked in black. Below it, written in flowing script, is the word Amduscias. Above it, *Madrigal of the World's End.*

It's the same unicorn I saw take form in ash

and smoke upon Gravetree's stovetop when last I was here. The same unicorn that *The Madrigal*'s first movement surely draws its name from. There is something deeply familiar about the image. Looking at it, I'm struck with a sort of atavism, as if I know it from another life and another time.

Returning to the task at hand, I sift through the sheets of paper on top of the piano, looking for pages from *The Madrigal*. I don't find the piece that my father and Gravetree wrote together. Instead, I come across many works by their subpar contemporaries sharing space with long-dead masters.

Turning my attention to the pages of music covering the floor, I kick aside snippets of concertos and sonatas. As I cross the room in this manner, looking for some sign of the song that haunts my mind, the fireplace catches my eye.

"No, no. no," I say aloud.

Atop of the charred logs lay blackened curls of paper and fine, dark ash. I fall to my knees, hurting them on the bricks of the fireplace, and reach my hands inside. The blackened cellulose crumbles at my touch. I sift through the carbon and ash and manage to find a scrap with a few notes intact. It's less than a bar, but I recognize the melody, a repeating theme from *The Madrigal of the World's End*.

"You son of a bitch," I mutter, struggling to breathe.

Dizzy, I rise and stumble toward the piano. I fall onto the bench, my mind reeling with fury and loss. Gravetree has betrayed my father and his legacy, just as Mother did. He destroyed one of the last pieces of him left in this world. I can find no forgiveness in my heart for that.

I look down at the pen-and-ink drawing of the unicorn on the ruined songbook. I stroke its mane with my finger and whisper its name.

"Amduscias."

The drawing comes to life at my invocation of its name. It shakes out its mane and ebony flames burst from inkwell eyes. It is majestic and terrifying and regal.

Keys on the piano slam down, possessed by some unknown power, and The Madrigal's *opening movement,* Goetic Prelude, *fills the air. A voice joins in, and though it whispers rather than sings, there is a musical quality to its words.*

"Your birthright is no more lost to fire's rage than the music was ever bound to page."

"Father is dead," I respond. "The scores are burned."

Chords form on the piano keys, and the foot pedals rise and fall of their own accord. Voices swell from the hallway. The portraits on the wall, Gravetree's hall of heroes, sing along with the piano. Samuel Barber's photograph belts out a beautiful baritone melody, while the watercolor of Liszt carries out a respectable tenor counterpoint.

"The score is gone, but the song does remain, if you dare to bleed it from Gravetree's brain."

Both the choir of portraits and the ghostly piano burst into hellish static at the notes I have missed, and they hit the bad ones I transcribed in error. They reveal nothing new.

The song is incomplete, but Amduscias, my regal unicorn, is right. There is one place *The Madrigal* still lives, and I might yet set it free.

The song ends as abruptly as it began, leaving me in silence.

I dislike silence.

"Amduscias, may I hear it again?" I implore.

"Of course, Master Beaumont," my *wondrous, equine nightmare whispers. "Your will be mine."*

The piano starts things off again, as I stroll out of the parlor. By the time I reach the hallway, the portraits have begun to sing once more, their various mediums deforming around their unnaturally animated mouths.

I make my way into the kitchen. Gravetree must have some booze. One cabinet reveals nothing, so I move to the next until I find a bottle of Cognac next to a collection of shot glasses. Each bears the name and a symbol of a European city. I choose Vienna, because how could I not? The liquor pours into the glass like liquid silk.

"I've found no words for *The Madrigal,* Amduscias. What is a madrigal without words?"

"Melodies are learned and forged in blood and tears and pain. The words will come to mind in time with sacrifice the same."

I throw back the shot of cognac. It barely burns at all. Gravetree's taste in booze is as fine as his taste in music. I pour another finger. With the bottle in one hand and a fresh shot in the other, I return to the parlor and take a seat on the piano bench. The sheet music atop the piano serves as a coaster for the booze. Condensation soaks into whole notes and double eighths.

The clock hands tick by, and the cognac grows shallow in the bottle, as I wait for Gravetree's return. *Amduscias keeps me entertained, repeatedly conducting the choir of portraits and the ghostly pianist in their incomplete rendition of* The Madrigal of the World's End. *Each time I hear it twin emotions mount—insane passion at the beauty of the music and maddening anxiety at its incomplete state. The feelings constrict around my soul, like twin serpents. My thoughts grow darker each time the song plays and with each shot I take.*

I'm angry but tired, and my mind is heavy with fog. I rest my head against the piano and close my eyes.

"Just for a second," I say, but it's a trap. In less than a minute, blackness overtakes me. My mind recedes into the realm of nightmare and dream. Fever visions of gallows, unicorns, and burning dancers play across the theater of my mind. Vivid fantasies of making love to Violet Sarkissian. Vivid fantasies of killing Violet Sarkissian.

Violet is straddling me, her sex engulfing my own. We float in an ebony void, surrounded by my choir on three sides, and Amduscias on the fourth. They are all dressed in matching black suits, save for Amduscias, whose equine head sits atop a human body decked out in a tuxedo.

One moment the choir is singing as Violet rides me. The next moment she is singing beneath me, in that incredible soprano, as I crush her throat with both hands. These visions strobe back and forth in increasingly short bursts. Violet is about to come. Violet is about to die. Then it all comes crashing down.

A slamming door wakes me. I lift my head from the piano, knocking over the bottle of cognac. Its final remnants spill across the scattered sheet music, adding to the condensation and my sleep-born drool.

My mind is foggy, and I struggle to banish the pain and dizziness. Gravetree walks past the parlor's entry, his arms full of grocery bags. He doesn't even glance into the parlor.

I grab hold of the bottle and stumble away from the piano. As quietly as I can, I sneak to the doorway. I stand to one side, pressing my body up against the wall, and I invoke the name.

"Amduscias," I whisper.

As if by magic, the piano comes to life.

Gravetree mumbles something from the kitchen. His voice is too low to make out, but I hear tension in it. I hear fear.

Slow, measured footsteps echo through his hall of heroes. Floorboards creak beneath his feet. The house betrays him with each step he takes.

Gravetree crosses the threshold, holding a meat tenderizer in one hand. *The music stops as he enters the room.* He's transfixed on the piano, and he doesn't see me. I strike out with cognac bottle. It shatters his wrist, and the spiked mallet skitters across the room.

He screams and falls in agony. From the floor, he turns his gaze toward me.

"You burned it," I say, my words slurred and

my tongue feeling unwieldy in my mouth.

I throw a handful of ash at him, burnt remnants of The Madrigal. *His skin blisters beneath its touch.*

"Lucien?" he asks, his face a mask of bewilderment.

"You consigned a piece of my father, something you created with him, to oblivion."

Gravetree skitters backward across the floor, slipping on his mess of papers. His hand reaches for the tenderizer. I throw the bottle down, narrowly missing his hand. It explodes in a shower of glass. Gravetree flinches. I take advantage of his moment of fear and retrieve the utensil myself.

"How could you do that to him?" I scream the question. "How could you do that to me?"

"Lucien, your father and I, we didn't write *The Madrigal of the World's End*. We uncovered it, like some pulp archaeologists stumbling into a cursed tomb. And believe me, it is a curse."

I take a step forward. He retreats further.

"That song is evil, boy. It's a dark, un-Christian thing, and its name is not hyperbole. It's the music of Hell, and it heralds the end of days!"

Gravetree's voice is high, his words pouring out in a jumble. He sounds like a madman or a street preacher.

"The end of the world, in my experience, is a microcosmic event," I say. "Not a grand-scale genocide but an old man murdered in his parlor."

Gravetree tries to find his feet, but his shoe slips on a piece of paper, and he falls back down on his ass. Tears run down his wrinkled jowls. He trembles and pisses.

"Amduscias is a devil, Lucien. That thing—that demon—killed your father!"

"My father killed himself."

I step over Gravetree, then fall upon him with all my weight. My knees pin his shoulders to the ground, and he blubbers like a child lost in the wilderness. I raise the meat tenderizer like a conductor's wand signaling a crescendo and bring it down with all the grace of the hammer man at a slaughterhouse.

Skin tears away from Gravetree's forehead. Blood runs like a river across the landscape of his face. He wails like an out of tune violin.

A thunderclap echoes in the room, signaling the choir of portraits to sing. They begin the familiar notes of Goetic Prelude in A minor, *Amduscias itself singing the parts which were earlier played on piano.* The Madrigal *is more than a collection of notes, though, and this time they sing the words.*

I lift the tenderizer again. Glistening blood drips from the metal spikes. My next swing comes sidelong, tearing a hole through Gravetree's cheek and shattering the teeth on his left side.

Amduscias keeps conducting, and the song reaches past the point that had been divulged to me previously. Missing notes reveal themselves, replacing the static emptiness with the fullness of music.

I hit Gravetree again and again, but I soften my strikes. This needs to take time. This requires patience and temperance. If I kill him too fast, I fear the music will stop.

My patience is rewarded. Amduscias leads the phantom singers through the entire prelude. Each strike of the tenderizer is like a metronome click, in perfect time with the music. When the last notes fade, an unresolved bit of discord, poor old Gravetree is unrecognizable. His white hair is dyed crimson, and shreds of skin hang from his face. His exposed cheekbones are fractured and broken. Shallow breath produces red foam from his broken nose and through his busted lips.

In the silence of the room, without the music playing, Gravetree's ruined face is too terrible to gaze upon. I roll off him, onto the floor, exhausted from the assault I just delivered. I allow myself only a few seconds of rest before rising. I must get to my songbook. I need to write down what I've heard before I forget it.

Once on my feet, I steal one more look at Gravetree. One more bloody bubble escapes his nose, then pops. After that there is nothing. His chest doesn't rise or fall. Neither his nose nor his mouth produces any more red mist or bloody effervescence. Philip Gravetree is dead at my feet.

I walk out to the kitchen and place the meat tenderizer in the dishwasher, nestling it between a half-dozen plates and cups. Next, I wash my hands and face in the sink, careful to wash all the blood down the drain. Once my hands are clean I start the dishwasher and return to the living room.

Gravetree is still dead, to my relief. I'd half expected to return to find some sort of phantom or wraith. That's crazy talk, of course, but one can do little to ward off imagination.

I don't want to be here anymore, but I fear to let another moment pass without transcribing the words and music. The price paid was too much to risk losing even one note or line.

My songbook is in my backpack. I retrieve it and take a seat at the coffee table, only feet from Gravetree's corpse, and transfer the music from my mind to the page.

SECOND MOVEMENT

DANCE OF DEPOSED KINGS

CHAPTER 8

I awaken in the darkness of my bedroom. Not the bedroom from the condo but my old room in the big house on Raylene Street. I know this, even though the room is oppressively dark.

Light pours in through the cracks of my doorway. From the other room I hear singing and mirth. Father's unmistakable tenor, along with another voice that I can't place. I yearn to be out there with him, with the music, the laughter, and the light.

My small fist tightens around the synthetic mane of my stuffed animal, and I carry it with me out of bed. A tidal wave of light hits me as I open the door. It hurts my eyes and blinds me for a few seconds. I squint and shield my eyes as I cross the threshold.

Looking to my left, I notice that the walls of the hallway are lined with two doors on each side, and the corridor terminates in a downward staircase. Glancing to the right, I see a single doorway at the far end—Father's office.

I make my way to Father's voice, which echoes from the other side of that far door. My bare feet make no sound on the soft strip of carpet runner that takes up most of the hallway's width. I find myself missing the softness of those fibers, even as I walk across it.

Father and the other man are still singing, the same part over and over again, with slight variations. The song is familiar, but I can't place it.

Eager to see Father's face—desperate to see it, as if I'll never again have the chance—I reach out and turn the knob. The door opens with ease, and inside sits Father at his desk, across from a man with unkempt white hair. Mother rests in a leather chair facing the northwest corner. She's smoking a cigarette with her back to everyone else.

They all look wrong, and so does the office. Father's head lolls to one side, and a noose trails down from his neck, the rope pooling beside his chair. The whites of his eyes are crimson with blood spilled from burst capillaries. Despite all this, and despite the blue/gray hue of his skin, he seems quite pleased.

The other man, the one whom I don't yet know as Philip Gravetree, sips tea with a ruined face. The Earl Grey pours from the inside of his mouth, out through rips in his shattered cheeks. Ruddy gore cakes his hair. Like Father, he seems undisturbed by his state of disfigurement.

Cracks zigzag down the yellowed Monet prints that are falling apart like ancient parchment in their frames. Books swell with moisture on crumbling shelves, and mold grows across their spines. Shot glasses overflowing with black venom litter the desk, alongside teacups bearing rust-

colored stains.

The only things to stand pristine are the baby grand and the score upon the music stand. I don't need to read the title on the sheet music to know what it says.

Father turns to me, that eerily familiar song on his lips, and he gives me a wink. The other man glances my way as well and raises his cup. The wounds covering his battered, torn face should make singing impossible. Nonetheless, a counterpoint to Father's own voice bellows out from the ruins of his mouth.

I grip my stuffed animal tighter, holding it close to my chest, and ask my mother for help. I'm not sure what I expect of her. To somehow turn Father back to normal? To restore this decaying, nightmare version of our home to what it was? It doesn't matter. She takes another drag from her cigarette and refuses to turn and look at me.

The dead men start their song over, repeating the same few measures again with a slight variation. I give them a wide berth as I approach the piano and the score sitting upon it. A black unicorn is scrawled across its cover, and the picture moves like some hellish animation as I open the book.

Father and Gravetree quit singing, and I hear papers rustling behind me.

"We'll never figure it out like this," Father says.

I open the book, and the pages are blank.

"Great art is not born without sacrifice, Philip."

I awaken in the darkness of my bedroom. Not the bedroom on Raylene Street but my new room in the condo. I know this, even though the room is oppressively dark.

The dream gave me nothing new. Not so much as a note.

It's been some time since I murdered Philip Gravetree. A week? Maybe two? I find it hard to keep track sometimes. But in that time I've added nothing new to *The Madrigal*.

"Great art is not born without sacrifice, Lucien," I say to myself.

No one else sits with us at lunch. Us, of course, refers to Maxwell, Asher, J. C., and myself. The Black Heart Boys' Choir. The name has begun to stick. Of course, the other students have come up with other names for our quartet as well, but none so apropos.

More than a week has passed, and I've figured out no more of *The Madrigal* in that time.

J. C. and Asher have taken to wearing full-on suits, cementing a uniform image among us. Asher maintains a bit of punk rock flair, pairing combat boots with slacks and sporting an array of accessories—gauche belt buckles, Texas ties, and bits of jewelry made from heavy chain and industrial refuse. J. C. sticks with a more basic look. Black suit. Black shirt. Black tie. Only a chrome belt buckle breaks up his dark uniformity.

More than a week has passed, and Amudiscias has been quiet, choosing not to reveal a single note or phrase.

We eat our lunches while discussing musical concepts and discussing pieces we might sing. We are still working on *O Magnum Mysterium,* and we are not tight enough to delve into anything much more complicated just yet, but it's entertaining to discuss. Maxwell suggests William Byrd's *Mass for Four Voices*. J. C. recommends adapting a choral arrangement of Glenn Danzig's *Black Aria,* and Asher wants to do something with percussion accompaniment.

I listen and consider their ideas, unable to make a suggestion of my own. The only song I can think of is *The Madrigal of the World's End,* and even if I held the complete work in my hands, I don't know that my choir is ready for it.

I don't know that I'm ready for it.

"We should skip next period and practice," I say. "We'll need to be tighter before we can move on to more complicated works."

"Sure," Asher says and chugs down the rest of his chocolate milk. "Why the hell not?"

J. C. nods in agreement, his mouth full of chicken nuggets. Only Maxwell hesitates. Poor, ever-nervous Maxwell. After a few seconds of inner struggle he agrees.

"I just have study hall, I guess. Screw it."

Asher slaps Maxwell on the back and tells him there might just be hope for him yet.

We finish our food, ignoring the occasional jibes of students walking by. Jokes about our clothes.

Jokes about our popularity and our sexuality. Jokes without humor and overflowing with malice.

It's five minutes before the bell when Ari Cole approaches our table. He's dressed in a Celtics jersey and faded blue jeans. I imagine he has and will dress nicer than that only a dozen times in his life. I don't know yet that he won't grow up—that we'll die on the same night—and I find myself speculating that he'll return to this same school after graduation as a gym teacher or a janitor.

He slams his palms down on our table and leans over. A sour expression crosses his face as he sniffs the air. Maxwell and J. C. stare down at their food, trying their best to ignore him. I glare at him, more angry than afraid, despite his gorilla-like physique.

"Man, it smells just like my piss over here!"

The table beside ours erupts into laughter. Ari leans in closer to me and sniffs again. He backs away, making an exaggerated show of disgust, and waves a hand in front of his face.

"Oh, that's my piss all right," he says, barely containing his own laughter. "Did you even wash that shit, man?"

"This isn't even the same suit," I say with no humor. Of course, it doesn't matter.

Other kids around at surrounding tables are spitting out drinks and slapping their tables as they crack up. They shout obscenities and insinuate that my hygiene is poor and that my suits come from Goodwill.

"Of course his suit smells," someone yells. "Probably the suit his crazy old man died in."

The laughing ceases, one person at a time, as the students begin to choke. They cough and spit, their food having turned to ash in their mouths.

Ari breaks into hysterics, no longer able to keep a straight face. A big, dumb smile stretches from ear to ear, and he looks like an ape laughing at a handful of his own shit.

"Seriously, bro, go see a dry cleaner or something."

Asher, who is leaning back in his chair and chewing an apple, stares Ari down and smiles. Ari's own smirk fades in response.

"Hey, Ari," Asher says, loud enough so all the tables surrounding ours can hear. "Tell your mom Derek's gonna be home on leave next month."

Ari's face is all rage now, his mean humor snuffed out by one sentence. The other baboons go quiet as well, except for the stray "ooh."

"You know, never mind. I'm sure she already knows."

Ari Cole strides toward Asher, throwing chairs aside as he walks. Asher stands up, cocksure and pleased with himself.

"I will fuck you up, freakshow," Ari snarls.

"That's no way to talk to someone who's practically your uncle," Asher says. "You should know that. I'm sure you've had lots of uncles growing up, after all."

Someone lets out a loud "oh shit," and Ari pulls his arm back to swing at Asher. Before he can throw the punch, a teacher's hand grips his shoulder.

"That's enough, Cole!"

Ari shrugs off the teacher's grip and backs

away from Asher. He points a finger at him, and it seems as if he wants to say something, but anger has stolen his words. The teacher ushers him away but not before warning that he'll be watching the four of us as well.

In less than a minute the lunchroom returns to normal. Kids get back to their conversations and their meals. The quiet gives way to the bee buzz of a hundred teenagers.

"What was that about?" I ask.

Asher, J. C., and Maxwell all break into laughter.

"Ari's mom is the biggest slam pig in town," Asher says. "She was working at Subway with my brother last year, before he went in the service, and some kids at school caught them banging in the bathroom."

"Fucking five-dollar footlong, baby!" J. C. adds, and we all laugh.

It feels good to be the ones laughing for a change.

It's Thursday at two in the afternoon, and while the rest of the school is learning how to take standardized tests and how best to prepare for a life of postmodern wage slavery, our choir has just nailed *O Magnum Mysterium* in the empty auditorium. No one fell out of time. Not one of us hit a bad note. And the power of our combined voices was something to behold.

It wasn't just music that we gave life to but

our combined lifetimes of disappointment and rage. Every bit of our pain and anger, reverberating off each other's and magnifying, exponentially.

They are almost ready for *The Madrigal,* I think. I'm almost ready for it. But not yet.

"I think that calls for a drink," J. C. says with a smile as we all sit with our legs hanging off the auditorium stage.

I return his grin and retrieve Father's flask . . . my flask now . . . and hold it up in the air.

"To an oasis of culture and intellect in this desert of mediocrity!"

The others clap and cheer. I take a swallow before passing the flask to J. C. It's my first drink of the day, and I'm happy to be sharing it with friends. I've spent too many days drinking alone over the past few months.

"Too bad we can't put on a concert or something," J. C. says, before taking a sip and passing the gin to Maxwell.

"We could do some recordings," Maxwell suggests. "Lucien and I have some equipment and software."

"Music like this, it loses something when you trap it in vinyl or computer code," Asher says, and I find myself nodding in agreement. "There's something about a live performance, something organic and visceral that you can't get in a recording."

"Let's just enjoy what we have," I suggest. "Singing for the sake of singing is enough for me."

Asher takes the flask from Maxwell and tips it to me. He takes a swallow and then studies the flask, tracing my father's inscribed initials and the iconography of a horse below them.

"Was this your old man's?" Asher asks.

I nod, feeling a lump in my throat at the mention of my father.

"It's cool that you have something like this to remember him by. Something that's practical and beautiful all at once."

He hands it back down the line. Maxwell and J. C. each take another drink before it gets back to me. I look down at the initials that I share with my dead father and let the smell of the gin coax pleasant memories of life before he passed. I love this flask, but it's not the treasure I want from Father. The only treasure I want is his song—the last bit of his essence I can scrape together.

"My old man's gone too, not sure if you knew that," Asher says, lying back onto the stage and speaking up at the array of lights above. "Prison, not the grave, but for all intents and purposes he might as well be dead. He left me something too. I'll show you sometime."

I don't say anything. There's nothing to be said, and I'm sure Asher understands that as much as I do.

"Mine had a heart attack when I was a baby. All he left me was a neurotic mother and a genetic disposition to be a fatass," Maxwell adds, patting his belly. We all snicker, Maxwell included.

"What about your father, J. C.? Is he in the picture?" I ask, passing the flask back down the line.

"Yeah, he's there, but he isn't much of a dad. Not much of a man at all. He's spineless, you know.

My mom walks all over him and cheats on him. My grandparents talk to him like he's a piece of shit. His boss takes advantage of him. He can't even bring himself to give me shit if he catches me smoking in the house."

J. C. takes a hard swig and shakes his head. There's a look of disgust on his face as he goes on about his father.

"He's all guilt and apologies. No matter what people do to him, he acts like he's in the wrong, and I guess he is for being such a pussy."

We sit and drink in silence for the next few minutes. We are all in our own worlds, haunted by the ghosts of our fathers and their individual failings. Looking out into the auditorium, I see the words *Fuck the patriarchy* scrawled in magic marker across a vinyl upholstered seat. I find myself mirroring the sentiment but probably not for the same reasons as whoever wrote it.

Fuck the patriarchy for decaying into a weeping, apologetic mass.

Fuck the patriarchy for falling into an aimless Peter Pan syndrome and shunning responsibility.

Fuck the patriarchy for looking for easy ways out and quick cash in lieu of hard work.

Fuck the patriarchy for walking into oblivion and leaving behind unfinished songs and unraised children.

No. That's all wrong. Fuck our fathers for not being patriarchs.

CHAPTER 9

It's Friday morning, and the sun is cresting the horizon. I'm supposed to bring a new song to the choir today. I want to show them *The Madrigal of the World's End*. I want to share it with them. I want to share it with the world. I haven't uncovered enough of the song, though.

I sip from a steaming mug of Earl Grey with a shot of bourbon and agonize over my notes regarding *The Madrigal*. I try to fill in the blanks of what I have. I try to compose something new to fill the missing movements. Nothing sounds right. Nothing is right. Single notes, arpeggios, and chords. Octaves, fifths, and discord. Nothing works.

Amduscias breathes in my ear. It tells me I know what must be done. Father whispers in the other, his voice raspy from the grip of his noose, telling me that there is no art without sacrifice.

I push the voices from my mind, focusing on what music I shall bring to my friends, rather than what I can't deliver. I turn over their suggestions in my head. J. C. wants to rearrange a neo-classical album by one of his favorite rock stars, but that would be too much work. I'm simply incapable of taking my mind off Father's madrigal for long enough to arrange a choral adaptation of a synthesized orchestral piece. Asher wants to do something with percussion, which I'm not crazy about, nor do I want to bring in an extra element just yet. Maxwell's suggestion is tailor-made for us, though. William Byrd's *Mass for Four Voices* will be our next piece. It's beautiful, with a sophisticated sound but a simple structure.

"You waste your time on dated masses. Secrets lie in mounds of ashes."

I push the words of Amduscias from my mind, and I wonder if the reason I'm reluctant to show *The Madrigal* to the choir is that it isn't ready for them, or because I'm not ready for it.

My name is called over the intercom. Not just mine. The static-addled voice also calls Maxwell, Asher, and J. C. (whom they call by his given name of Jesus, pronounced *Hey Zeus,* rather than *Jee-zus*).

I'm in Mr. Jackson's American Literature class when it happens. We are still discussing *The Scarlet Letter,* so it's no heartbreak to be called away. I am, however, curious as to why. We haven't done anything wrong, except sneaking a drink or two during the day, but that's not the kind of thing you get caught for after the fact.

Mr. Jackson excuses me, and I gather my things. My classmates let out the expected "ooh"s as I stand to leave. An effeminate voice with a practiced lisp comments that this looks like the end of the

Black Heart Boys' Choir. I turn toward the voice. It's Donny Hammond, the fashion queer from glee club.

He's wearing a rainbow ascot over a plain white T-shirt that bears the word pride across it in a massive, serif-free font. He acts as if it's pride that causes him to shout his sexuality out to the stars, but in truth he wears it like a cheap accessory from Claire's. Gauche and gay need not go hand in hand. I imagine Barber and Tchaikovsky would cringe just looking at him.

Hammond smiles at me and blows a kiss. A creeping sense of paranoia tells me that he knows something about why we've been called away from class. I straighten my tie and leave the classroom.

The halls are empty, and I take my time walking to the principal's office. I hope that I'll run into one of the others and that they might have an idea what this is about. No luck. I make it to the office without running into another soul. Maxwell, Asher, and J. C. are already waiting outside the principal's door.

They make room on the bench for me. I sit and ask if they know what's happening, why we've been called here. They don't.

After a minute of silence, Asher taps out a beat on the arm of the bench, a rapid march. Maxwell starts whistling a tune in time with it, some improvisation loosely modeled after Tchaikovsky's *Marche Slave.* J. C. and I smile at each other, and we each begin whistling our own improvised accompaniments.

It all begins rather softly, but in less than a minute we are making a great deal of noise. The office receptionist shouts at us to quiet down and asks us if we want more trouble than we already have. We stop the song, but her anger elicits a burst of laughter from J. C. which then spreads to all of us.

The woman glares at us from behind her desk, her growing rage fueling our laughter further.

The principal's door bursts open. Mr. Brodsky is standing there, looking more annoyed than angry. My mind immediately begins making comparisons between him and Mr. Larson from the Academy. Brodsky looks somewhat like Larson, in an emaciated, funny-mirror kind of way. Both men are balding, always dressed in suits, and have similar faces, but they are like night and day. Where Larson was an Armani man, Brodsky's clothes are wrinkled and cheap, lacking in any sense of elegance. Larson carried himself with military posture, his broad shoulders pushed back and square. Brodsky stands like an erect worm, his shirt bunching around his too narrow shoulders and stressing at the buttons over his belly.

He beckons us with one long, skeletal finger. His bushy, unkempt eyebrows furrow as he scowls at us.

"All four of you, in here now."

Maxwell's the first to his feet, despite his extra weight. He's used to people pushing him around, and he buys into the unwarranted authority of past generations. I can't muster up that level of respect for an old man in a shabby tweed suit and a novelty tie covered in yellow submarines, so I take my time rising. J. C. and Asher follow my cue.

We gather in Brodsky's office. He sits down

behind his cluttered desk. There are only two chairs on our side of the desk. It's a psychological tactic, not having enough chairs. He means to divide us and give those without a seat reason to feel ill toward those who do have one. Maxwell goes to sit, and I shoot him a glance. He retreats and stands in formation with the rest of us. We are one.

Brodsky gives us a sour look. He's disappointed that we didn't fall into his sloppy, amateur trap, but he doesn't push the issue.

"So I tell you to stop wearing suits, and you get all your friends to start wear them?"

"Is that why we're here, Mr. Brodsky?" I ask. "For not breaking the dress code?"

"Don't be a smartass, Beaumont," he snaps. "You're here because you've been using school grounds for an unsanctioned club. Your little choir or whatever."

"Someone ratted on us for singing in the auditorium?" Asher asks. "And you don't have anything better to do than give us grief about it?"

"Seriously," J. C. interjects. "Maybe you should focus on the football team shooting steroids in the locker room."

Brodsky does not seem moved by their arguments.

"If you gentlemen want to sing, join the glee club. There will be no more unsupervised meetings in the auditorium. There will be no more alternate music program."

"But don't you want to hear our song?" I ask.

Asher is the first to sing his part of The Madrigal. *J. C. and I join in after two measures, and finally, Maxwell follows suit.*

"Do you understand?"

Our vocals reverberate off the walls of the office, hitting the principal from every angle. The sound waves tear him to shreds, like a barrage of bullets cutting right through his body, only to ricochet and hit him again and again.

"Yes, sir," I say. The words feel cold coming out of my mouth. It pains me to speak them, as if they are a tangle of fish hooks in my throat.

I turn to leave. Maxwell, J. C., and Asher follow. None of us says another word to Brodsky nor do we wait to be dismissed.

"And for God's sake," he calls out after us, "get rid of those mafioso suits!"

We stop in the hallway once we are out of earshot of Brodsky and his secretary. J. C. coughs up a wad of mucus and spits in the direction of the office.

"At least they didn't bag us for drinking," Maxwell says.

"Someone ratted on us. I bet it was those glee club losers," Asher says.

He's right. It was the glee club. Probably Violet Sarkissian herself. I can see her in my mind's eye squealing on us. Her pouty, symmetrical lips telling Brodsky about our clandestine choir in her siren's voice.

I nod in agreement with Asher and tell them what Donny "Fashion Queer" Hammond said—that it looked like the end of the Black Heart Boys' Choir. J. C. scowls. Maxwell pouts. Asher slams the base of his fist into a locker.

"We need to get them back, J. C.," says.

"What we need to do is drag Donny Hammond out into the night and the fog," Asher replies.

I find myself thinking about Asher's proposal. Would Amduscias reward me if we took the boots to Donny Hammond? Would it reveal some piece of *The Madrigal* to me?

Maxwell is sweating and staring at the ground. This kind of aggression—this kind of anger—it's a stranger to him. I don't know how, considering the unkind manner in which the world has treated him.

"It's not that big of a deal, guys. I know some other places we can rehearse," he says.

"Oh yeah? Like where?" Asher asks.

It's just after three in the afternoon, and Maxwell is leading us down a set of rusted train tracks overgrown with weeds. This is the way to one of Maxwell's secret places, one of the places he comes to escape the cruelty and dumbness of this town. He brought me here over the summer, but it's out of the way, and we usually opted to hang out someplace easier to get to.

The arched boughs of trees form a canopy of red and yellow leaves, ready to fall in the weeks to come. Maxwell points out how the trees on either side of the tracks arch toward one another, forming a kind of vaulted ceiling. Walking through them feels like entering another world.

The annoyances of the school day evaporate into the fresh, clean air as we walk the tracks. The stink of Enfield recedes with every step we take into this forgotten place where dragonflies dart between flowers and chipmunks vanish beneath underbrush.

The pathway of trees opens into a clearing, and there in its center are the gorgeous, time-ravaged ruins of Enfield railway station. The place is a relic, from long before the MBTA forged its way out from Boston with their purple commuter rail trains. Boxcars and engines, as rich with rust as they are with history, sit beside the crumbling, façade of a train platform reclaimed by nature. The painted mural of the Boston and Albany Railroad Company's logo on the platform wall is faded and barely legible, like old watercolors on sun-bleached paper. Maxwell was right to pick this place. I'm hopeful that we might discover more here than dead locomotives and lost history by the day's end.

"Dude, this place is sick!" J. C. shouts, rushing into the clearing. Asher follows him, giving a nod of approval as he scans the derelict train yard.

"It's probably my favorite secret spot," Maxwell comments, happy to meet with approval from Asher and J. C.

"Man, even the graffiti's ancient here," Asher says, pointing to faded tags and sloppy, spraypainted logos for bands that no one remembers. "How does no one know about this place?"

"Because nobody goes exploring anymore. It's a lost art," Maxwell says. "Everyone's on their phone, so focused on getting a good picture of themselves that they don't notice the world around them. Luckily there's no such thing as a good picture of me, so I stopped trying and went looking for beauty elsewhere."

He pats his belly, and the other guys laugh, but I don't. There's so much more to Maxwell than his obesity. It saddens me that he defines himself by it.

I walk deeper into the clearing, stopping here and there to sing up and down the scale of C major. My voice is lost to the open wild and the blue sky above. I move closer to the platform, and my singing is deadened by the rotting wood. By the tracks, however, sandwiched between an old boxcar and a long-dead engine, the acoustics aren't half bad.

"It's not quite the auditorium, but I think it will do."

I sip from my flask, then offer it to Maxwell. He takes it and smirks like a child, pleased as punch that he's the one to save the day.

CHAPTER 10

"I heard you got into some trouble for using the auditorium without permission," Ms. Kane says, her voice flat and even.

I don't reply. This isn't a conversation I want to have right now. It's not something I want on my mind for the rest of the day. Still, just the thought of Violet fucking Sarkissian and her ignorant little clique ratting us out brings a burning flush to my cheeks.

"Do you want to talk about that, Lucien?"

Violet and her incredible, squandered talent. Violet and her crimes against music.

"Lucien?"

I don't answer. I'm afraid to answer. Afraid I'll cry. Afraid I'll hurt her. Afraid I'll cave her teeth in. Shatter that prostitute smile.

"Lucien!" This time she smacks her desk for emphasis. I catch her gaze and mumble something, though I miss my own words.

"You do understand that this wasn't a personal attack, right? It's just that you can't use the auditorium for an unauthorized, unsupervised club. It's against the rules."

"This administration cares about rules all of a sudden?" I ask. My words drip venom, and while my anger is really at Violet and the glee club, I find myself lashing out at Ms. Kane.

"Every class indoctrinates us into lawlessness. Art has no rules, it's all subjective. You tell us that third-world hellholes are the cultural equals of Renaissance Italy. In literature, we learn about Bob Dylan's Nobel Prize but never touch on Goethe, Milton, or Blake."

"Lucien," she interrupts, but I keep talking.

"Addiction's a disease. Gender is a spectrum. Race is a construct. You tell us that nothing is real, and then you speak of rules?"

"Those are false equivalencies, Lucien," she says with a calm that infuriates me.

"No, Ms. Kane. Calling a pop song glee club a music program is a false equivalency."

"Your problems with the material, your problems with society, even your problems with the glee club have nothing to do with this. The rules are the rules. You and your friends can't use the auditorium for a non-sanctioned club. I'm sorry."

She isn't sorry, though. Not one bit.

I sit back in my chair and huff like a child. I catch myself doing it and go red with self-loathing for such a weak display.

"I'm sure if you four really want to sing the glee club could make room for you."

Another huff of air escapes my lips, and I wave derisively.

"It doesn't matter," I say. "We found a new place to rehearse."

"Well, good. That means you can move past this," she says with that fake grin.

"Maybe we can talk about how you're otherwise adapting to the school? The friendships you're making or anything you're having a hard time with?"

"A hard time? You mean like Violet Sarkissian and her big mouth getting us kicked out of the auditorium? Or do you want to talk about how Ari Cole pissed all over my clothes, and I got in trouble for it?"

Ms. Kane is silent for a few moments. She jots something down on her yellow legal pad.

"If you want to talk about any of that, sure."

I reach out to the candy bowl on her desk and snatch up a Hershey Hug. She raises an eyebrow as I unwrap the candy and toss it in my mouth, as if she knows I only ate it to buy a few seconds where I won't have to speak.

"Or if there's something else you'd rather talk about?"

I take my time with the chocolate, letting it melt in my mouth. Ms. Kane waits for me to finish, never letting go of my gaze.

"I found some of my father's unfinished work," I say, having swallowed down the Hug. "Something that was never performed. It's a madri—" I stop myself, considering Ms. Kane's cultural ignorance, and alter my words accordingly. "It's a vocal piece, for four singers."

"And you and your friends were working on this piece by your father?"

"No," I shake my head. "We aren't there yet."

Grainy singing comes from PA speakers in the ceiling. Gravetree's voice. Father's voice. They sing a section from The Madrigal, *and the papers around the office ignite. Acrid smoke rises from Ms. Kane's computer monitor as the plastic frame blisters. The flames spread with incredible celerity, overtaking the legal pad in her hands and engulfing her hair. She is unmoved by the pain and shows no fear—no emotion beyond that paid for compassion. The expanding smoke burns my lungs as the world turns to ash around us.*

"But soon, I think."

It's after school, and Asher and I sit in his bedroom, passing my flask back and forth. J. C. had to go out for some uncle's birthday dinner or some such thing, and Maxwell is cramming for a test, so it's just the two of us today.

The walls are covered in pinned-up record sleeves, pictures of naked, tattooed women, and concert photos of musicians covered in spikes and streaked, monochrome face paint. The bands call it corpsepaint, I guess. To me, they look more like angry mimes than dead bodies.

Asher's mother is at work, and his father is in prison, so there are no adults here. I find comfort in this. I have no desire to be around the corrupt generations that preceded ours. Most of all, I don't want to go home.

"I'm telling you, we should just kick the shit out of one of them. Leave one of them with a wired jaw so they can't sing," Asher says, pulling a massive duffle bag from beneath his bed. "They took something from us, we should take something from them. You know what I mean?"

He unzips the bag and removes the contents. Inside is a rifle. I don't know much about guns, but it looks dangerous, like an assault weapon rather than something used for hunting deer. There's a beauty and elegance to its shape. The weapon is sleek and painted with a matte black that brings to mind a level of subtle class. The sight juts out from the barrel, like the single horn of a black unicorn.

"Remember I told you my dad left me something too? It's an M16 with a thirty-round mag. It's a fucking killing machine."

Asher hands me the gun. It feels good in my hands. I like the weight of it. I like the cold power that flows from it. It gives me that same chill that performing *The Madrigal* does.

"The glee club is supposed to perform at homecoming. What if we took that from them?" I ask. "Crashed it and *performed our own song?*"

My own words sound disingenuous. As if there is a disconnect between what I said, what I heard myself say, and what I meant to say. I try to sort it out, but *The Madrigal* blasts in my mind, denying me the clarity to do so. I give in to the music and let my mind swim in its cold embrace. The song pounds at the edges of my senses. It wants to escape. It wants to be shared.

"I have something else from my father— another inheritance of much greater value than this," I tell Asher, sloshing the liquor in my flask for effect.

"A song that no living soul has heard. A song imbued with magic to usher the end of worlds."

"Oh, yeah?" Asher asks. There is no trace of distrust in his voice. No mockery.

"But it's not finished. There are parts missing that I still need to find."

I stare down at the gun, dumbstruck by its simple elegance, and a revelation about *The Madrigal* strikes me. Asher has been pushing all along to incorporate drums into our music, and I scoffed at the concept, but *The Madrigal* is more than a song. It is magic and ceremony, and it needs a primal beat to power it.

"I think it needs some percussion."

I hand the M16 back to Asher. He smirks and grips it like a soldier.

"What's the end of the world without some brutal syncopation?" Asher asks, taking aim at an imaginary adversary.

CHAPTER 11

Music plays from Father's study, the same several measures, over and over again, like a skipping record. It is incomplete, neither starting out in a rational meter nor ending with any sense of resolution. I've never heard it before, but on some level I realize that this melody, and the suggested void on either side, will come to define me . . . consume me . . . devour me.

I stand on the other side of the closed door. It's an old door, like all the others at the house on Raylene Street, and it has an old-fashioned keyhole.

I grip my plush horse by the mane and peer in through the cutout in the brass plate. Inside the room, one of the bookshelves has been swung away from the wall, like an open door. On the wall, behind where the bookshelf should rest are a series of graphic photos.

In one is a gorgeous woman, engulfed in flame, mascara running down her agony-stricken face. Another shows a beggar hunched over, a crimson waterfall cascading from her open, ruined mouth. A third captures the final moments of a junkie, seizing in agony, surrounded by filth, needles, and pills. And the last picture is of a man in a fine suit, hanging from a gallows, the details of his face lost in shadow.

Musical notation marks each photo, drawn in indelible marker. Short snippets of static music trapped in scrawlings over static tragedies trapped in glossy cellulose.

Father paces, coming in and out of the narrow range of vision the keyhole affords me. He is crestfallen and his left hand taps out a rhythm, the sound of a plastic pen smacking notebook paper. His face, so like my own, bears the same frustration at his incapability of grasping The Madrigal *in its entirety. His eyes burn with the same hunger to hear the rest of the song, even just once.*

I squint, trying to read the music penned across the photographs, but it's no use. It's too far away.

"You just need enter and take a close look," a voice calls out. I shift my gaze toward the voice and see that my plush horse is alive in my hands, looking at me with knowing eyes framed by midnight hair.

"I don't have the key," I say in the voice of a child. "And it's not my place to enter."

"All treasures must be won by hook or crook," the stuffed horse says.

There is something terrible in the way that its toy mouth moves with the articulation of each word. I close my eyes, not wanting to see its unnatural, faux-equine features.

When I open them I find myself in bed, at the condo. My stuffed horse, the black one from my dream—the one I have had for as long as I can

CURTIS M. LAWSON

remember—lies next to me. It is still and quiet, just a toy. Just a toy, despite the shadow cast across the pillow, stretching from its crown like a horn made from darkness.

I lean over to look at my phone. It's eight in the morning on Saturday, and my shift at the record store starts in two hours. I need the money, so I can escape this place. I need the money, so I can leave Mother and this condo behind, so I can leave Violet and Ari behind, so I can leave Enfield behind. That's the plan, but part of me is aware that escape will never happen, not in the way I hoped. Some voice in my head laughs and screams, shouting that I'm caught in a decaying orbit. That I'm in the grip of this town's black gravity, where hope is sucked in like cosmic radiance lost to a singularity.

I send Jonas a text, telling him that I'm sick and won't be in today. I'd be surprised if he even bothers opening without me there, but that's his problem. My problem is *The Madrigal of the World's End* and its incomplete status.

I think back to my dream and wonder if it was fueled by memory. Did Father reveal *The Madrigal* in the same way I've learned to? The photographs on the wall of his office—were those the crimes . . . the sacrifices he made to Amduscias so that he might glimpse the music? Were the pictures still there, hidden behind the bookcase in his office at the house on Raylene Street?

I'll go there today, to the house on Raylene Street, and find out if any part of *The Madrigal* hides within the walls of my old home. There's another family living there now, but that doesn't matter. All that matters is the song.

It's Saturday afternoon, and I'm staring at my old home from across the street. The big house holds my fondest memories as well as the most painful. It hurts my heart seeing strangers eating breakfast through the glass walls of the conservatory and seeing unfamiliar cars parked in the driveway. It's like staring at the countenance of a dead loved one stretched and stapled across the face of some horror-movie lunatic.

The morning sunshine has vanished, and storm clouds cry above me. I stand below Father's umbrella. It's old-fashioned with a wide canopy, a long metal tip, and a curved mahogany handle.

A car drives by, kicking up plumes of water, and I catch my reflection in the tinted windows. Stick-thin and well-dressed, carrying an antique umbrella, I look like an Edward Gorey illustration in the imperfect mirror.

The car passes by, and the world is now monochrome, rendered in scratchy black ink with white, negative space. A cartoon cloud of dark exhaust trails behind the car and takes the equine form of Amduscias. The Black Unicorn gallops up the steep driveway to my old house, each movement a jerky bit of animation.

I chase Amduscias up the driveway, my knees pumping up to my chest in an exaggerated parody of genuine running. Raindrops patter off my umbrella. The precipitation is so uniform and symmetrical, one might guess it was drawn with a ruler. White ringlets radiate around my feet with each step, displacing the India ink darkness of the wet driveway.

Amduscias comes to a halt beneath the willow tree in the front yard, the one with the heart-shaped scar in the bark. I follow the demon under the shelter of the tree's drooping foliage and close Father's umbrella. I trace my fingers across along the bark, across the writing in the center of the carved heart.LB³, it says. Louis Beaumont. Lindsey Beaumont. Lucien Beaumont.

Hidden by the low-hanging boughs and oppressive rain, I stare in at the new family living in my home. A young girl works on a school project at a dining table in the conservatory. It looks like a science experiment of some kind with miniature Tesla coils arcing white lightning bolts and cross-hatched mist billowing from beakers. Her mouth is moving, but the parents ignore her and each other. The mother is focused on a martini and her laptop, while the father paces in a tight circle, chattering into a cell phone.

As close as they are, all in the same room, they are worlds apart. I suppose that's what passes for family these days. I'm not about to complain, though, as this works in my favor. With the three invaders all together on the east side of the house, I'm free to sneak in through the basement.

The unicorn nuzzles my neck before vanishing into wispy smoke. Frost forms in my veins at its touch. It steels me for what might come next, for what I'll have to do if they catch me.

I tiptoe around the house, passing along the

western side, opposite the conservatory, my back arched over like a bow and my knees raising up to the same ridiculous heights as when I'd been running up the driveway. The greenery of the back yard I grew up in, like the rest of the world, has given way to inky darkness set against a vacuous field of white. This place has died without us there to tend it. Or maybe I'm dead without it. Either way, the house on Raylene Street is haunted, and I'm an angry ghost stalking the grounds.

The bulkhead is locked, but this new family never fixed the basement window, the one in the back that never latched. I pull, and it offers no resistance. The opening is small, but so am I. I drop my umbrella in through the window, then slither through, feet first.

All is darkness in the basement, save a stream of light coming in diagonally from the window. Crisp, straight borders separate the light from dark. I crouch down, feeling for the umbrella. There are a few moments of anxiety as I worry my hand might find a rat or a spider instead, but such thoughts flee at the familiar texture of the curved mahogany grip.

With Father's umbrella in hand, I step beyond the wedge of radiance, and my body is lost in a sea of brush-rendered gloom. I navigate the basement by memory, hoping these intruders haven't cluttered the place with useless junk, and to my luck they haven't. I find the stairs with only a few bumps.

White light from the other side outlines the door at the top of the steps. I ascend toward it, light on my feet. I skip the third step from the bottom completely, remembering how badly it creaks. If they hadn't fixed the window, I doubt they fixed a noisy board on the stairs.

When I get to the door, I press my ear against it and listen for any noise. I hear the family, but it sounds as if they are still rooms away, over on the east side of the house. The basement lets out below the foyer stairs, over on the south side.

The knob turns freely in my hand, and I step out into the empty foyer. It looks different. Plain white walls with hastily sketched pen-and-ink family portraits occupy space where there used to be Impressionist prints set against burgundy paint.

My own breath sounds thunderous in my ears as I creep toward the front of the staircase. Each step is slow and measured—precise, light movements of ball to heel. I turn and place my foot on the bottom step, terrified it will creak—that my house will betray me to the parasites infesting it. The wood gives no protest. The entire way up the only sound is the slightest click of my shoes against the wood, but the new family can't hear that from rooms away.

The hallway at the top of the stairs stretches in two directions. To the right are the bedrooms, whose doors now seem crooked and misshapen, perfectly fit for their crooked, misshapen frames. I turn left and make my way to the room that had once been my father's office. Like the other doors and frames, the entryway to this room is also slanted and out of square. Instead of a rectangle, it's in the shape of an old-fashioned wooden casket, the kind of thing you might see in a spaghetti western or a horror film, but if the prop guy had been a lush and made it asymmetrical.

I jiggle the doorknob, to find that the room is locked. A piece of tattered string hangs down from the handle, terminating at the fat, rounded top of the old-fashioned keyhole. It looks like a hangman's silhouette. It makes me afraid.

Amduscias forms behind me. Its cold snout presses against my ear, and it whispers.

"You just need enter and take a close look."

"I don't have the key," I say in a voice so much like my father's. "And it's not my place to enter."

"All treasures must be won by hook or crook," the unicorn says.

I swallow back my fear and turn to face Amduscias. Its inky, hellfire eyes bore into me, and I let its gaze burn my soul. The demon silently offers to help me through the gate but not without a sacrifice.

I press my index finger to the unicorn's mouth. It licks, then nibbles, and finally devours the flesh. I grind my teeth until they crack, trying to silence my pain. When all the meat is gone, Amduscias chews at the bone, sculpting the tip of my finger into a skeleton key. The demon pulls back its head and licks the ebony blood and alabaster marrow from its mouth and beard before dissolving into the ether.

My mutilated finger slides into the mortise lock. With a flick of my wrist, the lock throws open and clicks. The door opens to a sketchbook version of Father's office. Rudimentary inked imitations of his furniture, his piano, and his bookshelves. These things can't be here, I find myself thinking. Mother sold his piano and his desk. On the bookshelves, I see books of his—books that can't be here because they line the shelves at our condo. And yet . . .

I caress the curves of the piano with my left hand, the one spared the hunger of Amduscias. My fingers dance across the dark flats and sharps, taking pleasure in their smooth texture and the feeling of tension and weight beneath them. I want to press down and make them sing, but I dare not alert the family of vermin to my presence.

In a gesture of love, I press two fingers to my lips, my skeletal index and my intact middle, then lay them upon the piano before turning back to the task at hand.

The bookshelf from my dream, the one that hinged away from the wall, is burdened under the weight of dozens upon dozens of hardcovers, paperbacks, and spiral-bound volumes. Despite the load it bears, the bookshelf swings away from the wall with ease. Behind it, I find the photographs, which are now more like sketches, still stuck to the wall. I snatch them, one by one. They are all here— the burning bitch crying her makeup off, the beaten street urchin, the dying addicts. On each of them, someone has written a bar from The Madrigal of the World's End. *Each holds a part of the song that I have not yet revealed.*

I clutch them to my chest, then tuck them into my breast pocket. With my treasure in hand, I quickly make my exit from the room. When I get back to the top of the stairs I listen. There are footsteps and mutterings heading toward the front of the house. I duck back into the threshold of one of the rooms near the stairs. From here I still have a decent vantage point of the foyer, but if they look up, they will also see me.

The father of this family, a man in a tacky business-casual weekend outfit of cargo shorts and a polo shirt, a man so unlike my own father, leads his wife and child toward the front door. The mother keeps typing away at her phone, ignoring her husband's rants about making the most of the weekend. The daughter glares at the floor, lost in the desolation that is her family. She stops for a moment, falling behind her parents, and looks up at me. There is a yearning in her gaze as if she's asking me to release her from all this.

The front door opens, and the father walks out, leaving my home. Then the mother. Finally, the daughter approaches the doorway. She glances back at me again with tears in her ebony eyes, then steps across the threshold, out of my home and into the gray day beyond. The door closes behind her.

With the family gone, I stand up and take a deep breath. I'm trembling as I walk down the steps and make my way to the door. I wait a few minutes, just enjoying being home again, and giving the intruders time to put distance between us.

When I finally walk out the front door, a cloud moves away from the sun, and I am struck by its light. Black ink washes away like rain, revealing the real, full-color world beneath, in clear, high definition.

The black blood covering my hand has turned red, and my finger is intact save for lacerations in the shape of a human bite. Crimson splatters decorate my blazer, shirt, and tie. The metal tip of my umbrella drips real-life blood onto wet pavers. I'm not sure where the blood came from. I'm not sure why it's there.

I reach for my breast pocket searching for the photographs. Instead, I find drawings, in the shape of Polaroids, rendered from black pen with red and orange crayons. Bars of music are scrawled across each.

"What's happening?" I ask aloud, turning back to look at the big house on Raylene, as it really is, rather than as an Edward Gorey sketch.

"What matter are whos or hows or goddamn whens? Just know that bloodshed sings the song of this world's end," Amduscias sings from all places and none at the same time.

"What are you?" I ask, unsure if the question is for Amduscias or myself.

The steam-covered mirror of the bathroom obscures my face as I towel myself dry. I wipe away the condensation and examine myself. I turn my head back and forth, up and down, looking for any tenacious crimson stains hiding behind my ears or in the creases where my nostrils meet the flat of my face.

There's no blood, but I can still feel its heat and its slick stickiness. The feeling makes me sick, and I fight the urge to retch.

Once dry I head to my room and lay out new clothes to replace the gore-stained outfit I had to dispose of. I choose a cool pallet, grey pants with a purple shirt and black tie. Cool colors calm me.

I cast my towel into the hamper and stream music through my phone—The Best of Paganini. Violins play as I get dressed. I'm careful to line up the centers of my clothes and maintain just the right tuck of my shirt. One should take pride in one's appearance, even in the worst of times.

With my clothes on and the passionate compositions of Paganini playing in the background, I find myself asking the same question I asked outside the house on Raylene.

"What are you?"

This time I'm sure that it's Amduscias I'm referring to.

My phone begins buzzing. There's a text from Maxwell, telling me that something happened at my old house. Someone broke in and killed the whole family. Wife. Husband. Child. I throw up in my mouth but swallow it back.

I'm lucid for the first time in a while, and as such, I feel angry.

I think about Gravetree and what I did to him. Did I do that? Did I actually murder him?

I think about the family I don't remember killing at Raylene Street and my wild, monochrome hallucinations.

I think about my dream of Father killing my mother's junkie lover all those years ago, and I can't tell if it was memory or fiction.

It all sickens me, in the most literal way, and it all leads back to the song and the unicorn.

Instead of texting Maxwell back or inventing an alibi, I turn my attention to Amduscias. I search the name online, finding a few variations on the spelling—Amdusias, Amukias, and Amdukias. Almost every site says the same thing, a quotation from the Lesser Key of Solomon. I whisper it to myself as I read.

"The sixty-seventh spirit is Amduscias. He is a Duke great and strong, appearing at first like a unicorn, but at the request of the exorcist he standeth before him in human shape, causing trumpets and all manner of musical instruments to be heard, but not soon or immediately. Also, he can cause trees to bend and incline according to the exorcist's will. He giveth excellent familiars. He governeth twenty-nine legions of spirits."

Illustrations of anthropomorphic unicorns with midnight coats abound in the image search. They blow into brass horns and float in whirlwinds of musical notation. Sites dedicated to Goetia, which I discover is the magic King Solomon used to summon demons, refer to the creature as the infernal conductor, and the muse of the damned.

I study the ink and crayon drawings from Father's study, those static moments of suffering, laid out on my nightstand. I consider the notes penned across each and hear their haunting bars in my head.

"Amduscias, I invoke thee." My voice is possessed of a quiet forcefulness. "I demand the truth. About my father. About *The Madrigal*."

Thunder sounds outside, as if in answer to my summons. Ebony clouds billow from beneath my bed, like Hell fog rolling in from a brimstone sea. The mist grows and rises. A mass erupts before me—the ethereal darkness taking on form and substance. Amduscias rises, a nightmare version of a shape in the clouds. Its eyes burn with the orange luminescence of smoldering charcoal.

"You have questions, young Master Beaumont?" the dark god asks me. "You want to know the things you know not."

Its voice is beautiful and terrible.

"What is *The Madrigal of the World's End*?"

"Just what it seems and just what you seek here. Armageddon, packaged in melody and meter."

Those terrible, burning coal eyes keep my gaze bound. Smoke sears my lungs, and tears stream down my cheeks.

"Did my father write it with Gravetree, or did you reveal it to him, as you did with me?"

"Dead masters wrote it, one thought and deed at a time. Now it's yours to compose with each dream and each crime."

"What happened to my father?" I ask. "Did he kill himself because of the things he did in your service?"

"He's trapped in the notes. Same as you. Same as me. Finish the song, and we'll all be set free."

"Did you kill my father?" This time I scream the question.

"To call your father dead is truth cut in half. His best parts live on in blood and stave."

I pull at my hair and scream, frustrated and angered with the demon's roundabout rhymes. *It lets out a musical laugh, amused by my displeasure.* I wipe the tears from my face and take deep, calming breaths so I might ask it the most important question I can think of.

"Are you real?"

I'm met with silence and an empty room. There is no billowing cloud. No black unicorn. Just me.

CHAPTER 12

It's Sunday, and I'm at work. I still feel sick from yesterday. Sick from the feeling of blood and the vertigo of hallucination. Pain throbs from beneath the bandage on my finger. The small bite from the teeth of someone not yet fully grown, now hidden under gauze and adhesive plastic.

It's Sunday morning, and I don't know if black unicorns exist, or if I'm mad, or if I'm a killer. I don't even know that one necessarily precludes the others. I have no memory of killing that family on Raylene Street, but someone did. It's all over the news. But I did kill Gravetree, didn't I? I can't find his obituary online. Has no one found his body yet?

The record store is empty, a small mercy that I fully appreciate. Not even Jonas is here, which comes as no surprise. I wonder if he even opened the shop yesterday without me here. It doesn't matter, I suppose, unless the cops come around asking questions.

Where were you yesterday, Mr. Beaumont?

I stepped into a pen-and-ink, Edward Gorey version of my old house where that family was murdered.

Did you kill them?

No, no. I simply snuck in through the basement and broke into my father's old office to steal violent drawings marked with musical notation. I know it sounds bad, but it was at the insistence of the sixty-seventh Duke of Hell.

I shake the imaginary encounter from my head and look down at my songbook. There is nothing I can do about yesterday, but I can still figure out this damn song.

The drawings I found, the ones that mirror the photographs from my dream, are laid out across the counter. The notations written on each must fit this score somehow. I should be able to figure out where in the song they go or make a damn good guess at least. I mark down the keys above each, which allows me to place them within the proper movements.

The bar scrawled across the image of the hanging man is in A minor, same as *Goetic Prelude,* and it fills the final lost measure of *The Madrigal*'s opening. That snippet of music that I copied from the picture of the bleeding vagrant is a variation on a theme from the first movement, *Black Unicorn Sonata.* The bar could fit into either of the two spots still missing in the first movement, and it occurs to me that it might repeat and fill both. I pencil the notes into my songbook over both empty measures.

Next, I study the bit of music accompanying the picture of the dying drug addict. Six eighth notes make up the bar, which would seem to indicate waltz timing. That places it in the second movement. There are, however, too many missing spots on that section of the score to guess where this slice of song might fit.

I hum each of the four parts from the second movement, one measure at a time. I tap out the waltz beat on the counter, one, two, three, one, two, three. There's a sadness to the melody, and a sense of loss, but also prideful anger. It's not a waltz intended for lovers to hold each other close but rather a dance of deposed kings.

Dance of Deposed Kings. That feels right, and it invokes the same cold sensation that overcomes me as when I play or sing a selection from the piece. I scrawl the words into my songbook, next to where it says "Second Movement."

I go back to my tapping and humming. At each void in the score, I insert the notes from the drawing, hoping they fit so perfectly that there can be no doubt of their placement. That doesn't seem to be the case.

Frustrated, I move on to the picture of the gorgeous, burning woman. The notes on this image make no sense, though. They follow no scale. The measure is an ugly mess that doesn't fit anywhere. But there were pages torn out from Father's copy of the score. They must have contained a final movement. Some sort of atonal fantasia perhaps?

A ringing bell—the sound of a customer entering the store—pulls my mind away from *The Madrigal.* I lift my gaze and see that it's only Maxwell. I cover the pictures with a jewel case from the counter and wave hello.

"What are you working on?" he asks, approaching the counter. "Something original?"

I shrug and wave my hand across the pages

of the songbook. I'm unsure how to answer. Does this belong to my father and Gravetree? Is it something much older, composed by some king of the pit? Or did the demon speak the truth when he said *The Madrigal* was mine now?

"I decided to finish what my father began. The piece he composed with Gravetree."

Maxwell motions toward the songbook, seeking permission to touch it. I nod, and he turns it around so that it's right side up from his perspective across the counter.

"This is fucking wild, Lucien," Maxwell says, his voice full of excitement. He hums a few bars, and his smile widens. "For real, this is awesome. I mean, it's dark, but it's beautiful. Is it for the choir?"

"Yes. I think so. Not yet, but it will be."

Maxwell flips through the pages, a look of confusion replacing the excited expression he wore just before.

"There are still random, missing bars. Are you jumping around as you compose it?"

"That's my process. I've found a sense of muse, and it leads me to where it likes in the song."

My words are true if missing some detail.

"Well, whatever your process is, it's working." He hums a few more bars, smiling again. "This is so good, dude!"

I find myself wondering if Maxwell would feel the same if he knew the truth of "my process." He's so good-natured that I wonder if he'll still be part of this when I tell the choir the truth. Would he understand the need to sacrifice, in a biblical manner, for the creation of something this wondrous? Would he find beauty in its melody if he knew it was the product of blood and madness?

The bell rings again. Maxwell and I both glance over at the door, and my heart catches in my throat. Violet fucking Sarkissian is walking into the record store. Even with the giant, bug-eye sunglasses she's wearing, the girl is unmistakable. Her full, pouty lips. Those long raven curls, as dark as the mane of Amduscias. The inhuman symmetry of her features. All that physical beauty, and it is still mundane compared to the majesty of her voice.

God, I fucking hate her.

One of her glee club friends follows behind— the dumpy girl with the kinky hair, who had given a dismal performance of a Disney tune at the tryouts. Violet is berating the girl under her breath, a disgusted sneer etched upon her lips. The dumpy girl is frowning and slinks behind Violet like an omega wolf slinking behind the alpha bitch.

"Hi, Violet," Maxwell says with his typical gregariousness and complete lack of self-awareness. "Hi, Ashley," he adds, this time with nervous tension underscoring his tone.

Violet snarls at him. The dumpy omega girl, who I guess is named Ashley, waves at Maxwell and gives him a smile before Violet shoots her a disapproving glance. Ashley puts her head down and turns away from Maxwell.

It's just as well that Violet played the role of bitch there, squashing any awkward, fat-kid infatuation the two might have fostered. I wouldn't want Maxwell fraternizing with the enemy, and

Violet just saved me from having to be the bad guy.

I take the songbook back from Maxwell and slap it closed. *The Madrigal* is not for the eyes of plebeians, and I fear that even their glances upon the sheet music could taint its majesty.

"May I help you?" I ask, in my most insincere customer service voice.

Violet glares at me from behind her big, bug-eye sunglasses and lets out a practiced mean girl laugh. It's evil, and infuriating, and sexy. It makes me want to break her, and kiss her, and love her, and cut her throat from ear to ear.

"Doubtful," she says and strolls over to the section of vinyl new releases.

The two go back to their conversation, while Violet flips through pop records that I would barely qualify as music. Violet is giving the girl shit about her performance at glee club practice. After hearing her sing the once, I'm sure she deserves the grief.

I'm actually a bit impressed that Violet is concerned with the quality behind the glee club. My impression had been that it was all for fun and that she was perfectly content shining above her untalented peers.

"I don't care if you want to give a shitty performance during the rest of the show, but if you fuck up backing my solo at the Homecoming dance, I'll see to it you're as miserable as those losers for the rest of the year." She gestures toward Maxwell and me as she says this.

"I'll practice more," Ashley mutters, looking small and ashamed. "I'll get it right."

"You better," Violet says, examining an LP

featuring a woman's face smeared with glittery makeup on the cover. "The recording of this is going to be my ticket to New York, and I am not going to let you turn it into some basic bitch high school performance."

New York? It never occurred to me that anyone else in this bullshit little town might have aspirations for something more. I mean, I'm sure plenty of them will try to get into a party college far enough away from Mommy and Daddy to drink and drug to their heart's content, but most of them will come back here to settle down and mate, like spawning salmon. But Violet, it seems, wants more.

I suppose it makes sense. Her beauty. Her talent. The profound fucking blackness of her heart. It's all too much for Enfield to hold within its limited grasp. I suppose we have more in common than I thought.

"Well, stop following me around then and go practice," Violet says to Ashley, shooing her away like an insect.

Ashley mumbles her assent and skulks out of the store, ringing the bell as she leaves. Violet doesn't bother to turn away from the records.

I watch as her pristine, lacquered nails flip from one record to the next. I concentrate on her voice, as soft singing carries from her lips. I hunger for the dimensions of her body as she subtly dances to the music in her mind.

"Hey, Lucien," Maxwell says, reminding me that he's still in the store—reminding me that anyone or anything other than Violet Sarkissian exists. "I need to drop a book off at the library. You wanna meet up later?"

I turn to him and nod, though I don't mean it. I don't want to meet up with Maxwell later. I want to make love and hate to Violet while the choirs of Hell sing *The Madrigal of The World's End*.

"All right, see you later. And great work on your dad's piece," he says as he exits the shop.

There is no music playing over the speakers, as I had been concentrating on my own project. I can't go back to *The Madrigal* with Violet in the store, though, so I put on Debussy's *Clair de Lune*. My hope is that its simple, calm beauty might quell my hunger for both the girl and *The Madrigal*.

Violet snorts in derision as the first piano notes play from the vintage speaker cabinets in each corner of the store.

"This is why you have no customers in here," she says,

"A fact that clearly leaves me heartbroken," I reply.

Deciding on a record from some pretty boy who looks more like a model than a musician, she approaches the counter. I wonder if Debussy's subtle, *pianissimo* style spurred her to a quicker decision. If I had played Wagner perhaps she would have run straight out of the store.

"Seriously, why are you so weird? The suits? The classical music? Your nerd choir with your creepy death rock friends?"

I scan the record, and the model-handsome singer smiles up at me with gleaming white teeth and unearned confidence. I don't have to listen to the record to know that it's garbage music, manufactured for the lowest common denominator—the artistic equivalent of a suit from Walmart or a bottle of Seagram's Extra Dry.

"Normal is common," I say. "People of exceptional talent and ambition should strive for more than normal," I tap the record as I accentuate the last word. "But I suppose exceptionality mustn't always go hand in hand with good taste."

"Whatever, virgin," she says, pulling a Coach wallet from her Coach purse. As she looks down to retrieve her cash, I catch a glimpse of her eyes beneath her sunglasses. An angry brown and purple bruise is hiding behind the oversized shades.

A righteous anger wells up in me at the sight of Violet's black eye. Someone hit her? In the face? Yes, I want to love her and destroy her, but the thought that someone might actually hurt her— someone other than me—is inconceivable. It's like smashing a Michelangelo or burning a Titian.

She sees me staring, realizes that I've caught sight of her black eye, and pushes her glasses back up the bridge of her upturned nose. I'm paralyzed for a moment, gripped by anger at the thought of someone striking her, some apish jock boyfriend or callous-handed, blue-collar father.

"What happened to your eye?" I ask. "Did someone do that to you?"

She shoves her money across the counter, and her lips curl into a dangerous snarl as sexy as it is venomous. "What the fuck do you care? Mind your business, weirdo."

Fuck her, I think. *The bitch deserves more than a slap.*

I don't mean it, though. She's a work of art—an exceptional, beautiful person trapped and poisoned by the soul-sucking anomie of our age and the black hole gravity of this town.

I take her money and count back her change. She shoves the bills and the coins into her purse without counting them, then storms off with her record before I can put it in a bag.

There is an intentional confidence to her stride as she leaves the store. She walks with grace. She walks like royalty, determined not to succumb to the mediocrity that surrounds us.

We are the same, I realize. I find myself hoping that Violet does make it to New York. I find myself hoping that we both escape Enfield.

CHAPTER 13

"Why does the world detest greatness, Ms. Kane?"

The question is not my usual deflection or some passive-aggressive attempt to bait her. It's sincere. I want to know why my father was driven to madness and stuck his neck in a noose. I want to know why Ari Cole and his asshole jock friends try to snub out the flame of intellect and creativity in people like myself and my choir. I want to know why some piece of shit would leave Violet with a black eye, even though I want to do so much worse to her.

Ms. Kane taps her pen against a legal pad and considers my question. Her typical, I'm-paid-to-be-here smile is absent. Instead, she wears an expression of genuine consideration. I hope she has an answer. Not just an answer but a solution to the problem—something practical and workable. I just want one fucking adult in this dumpster fire of a world to be able to tell me how to fix a problem. Isn't that why they're here?

"I think that a great many people fear what is exceptional, Lucien. I think they are scared of being

137

left in the dust and sometimes lash out because of that."

I nod my agreement. I see no flaw in her insight, but it holds no solutions.

"Does this have to do with getting kicked out of the auditorium or your problems with the glee club?"

"Partially, I guess, but it's more than that," I admit. "Do you remember I told you that I found an unfinished piece by my father?"

"I do."

"What I didn't tell you is that my mother had tried to destroy it. She painted black ink across the bars on every page, trying to erase my father's last piece of genius from the world."

Ms. Kane rests her pen on her pad and leans toward me. A sad smile stretches across her lips.

"I don't think your mother is trying to destroy your father's legacy or undermine his achievements. You need to remember that she lost a lot when your father died as well. It's not uncommon for a person to lash out at a deceased spouse after a suicide. There are a lot of difficult emotions to deal with there."

"She was supposed to be the grown-up," I say. "She was supposed to keep it together."

"Lucien, I'm going to let you in on a little secret. Most grown-ups aren't all that grown up. We manage to pay the bills, hopefully, and some of us learn to avoid drinking until work is over, but other than that we mostly make it up as we go along."

Her tone is tragically honest and matter-of-fact. She's probably right, but that doesn't make it acceptable. Things couldn't have always been like this. How could humanity have made it this far if every generation had been a rudderless, neurotic mess?

"Even if she is lashing out at my father, why squash her own greatness? I haven't heard her sing at all since he died. Not once. She hasn't done a damn thing but pop pills and drink in her room."

Ms. Kane seems concerned. She places a hand over mine.

"Lucien, are you not being taken care of at home?"

"I can take care of myself, and I'll be out of there by July," I say.

"Well, if you don't feel safe at home . . ."

"It's fine," I assure her.

There is a moment of quiet as Ms. Kane scribbles something down on her legal pad. Probably a note about my home life. I should have kept my mouth shut. The last thing I need is social services digging around.

"Back to the idea of greatness. You feel that the world is trying snuff out yours?"

"Maybe not the world but certainly the town of Enfield. And not just me, either. It's like the smallness of this place is contagious. Ari Cole pisses on my clothes, and I slink away like a weasel. Then I seethe for hours and days, getting angry at everyone and everything—people who I've never met and who have done nothing to wrong me."

"Those people were intruders, and Gravetree was a betrayer," Amduscias whispers into my ear. *"You did just what you had to do to be your family's savior."*

I ignore the phantom voice and focus on Ms. Kane's intense hazel eyes.

"And that anger—that hate—it drains so much from me. Instead of composing or working on my escape plan for next year I just sit there and daydream, this awful, vengeful stuff. And not just against the jocks or the glee club. Not just against Mr. Brodsky or my mother. Against anyone stuck in the decaying orbit around this town."

I can feel the hairs of Amduscias' beard caress my neck. Its breath is hot against my cheek.

"Now you're just being dishonest, with her, yourself, and me. That hatred—that violence—is the only art you've worked on since July."

"It's easy to feel that everyone is against you, Lucien," Ms. Kane says. "There will always be bullies, and you often won't get your way, but the world isn't your enemy. Try to focus on the things you most want. And your real enemies? The people who genuinely want to cause you harm? Leave them in the rearview mirror."

"What is it you most want, young Master Beaumont?" the demon's voice asks. In the background I hear the choirs of Hell singing Father's madrigal . . . my madrigal.

Students cram the halls, all trying to escape from school as fast as they can as if the teachers might call us all back if we're too slow. I swap out books from my locker and give my bobblehead Beethoven a slight nudge, eliciting a wild, broken-necked nod from the plastic composer. I don't have work today, and I'd rather not go home yet, so I scan the halls for my friends. Instead of Maxwell, J. C., or Asher, I run into Violet. She's by herself—a rarity—and she puts her head down as she passes by without an unkind word or an insult.

Perhaps she saw in me what I saw in her yesterday, that we are very much the same. Maybe a crack of empathy formed in each of our black hearts.

There is still no sign of the choir, so I shut my locker and follow Violet, keeping a safe distance between us. I'm not even sure why I'm following her, but I imagine she wouldn't be happy if she realized it.

The crowd parts around her, like peasants making way for royalty. I am not met with the same courtesy, instead having to push, nudge, and maneuver my way through the throngs of high schoolers.

When she's only yards away from the front door I lose her in the crowd. I push past football players and burnouts, through circles of girls giggling at their phones and past teenage activists hanging posters for causes they don't understand. Finally, after bumping around the crowd like a human pinball, I make my way outside. I've lost Violet in the sea of students descending on the parking lot. I scan the crowd, trying to pick her out. It shouldn't be tough. She's a goddess among insects.

A hand touches my shoulder, and I spin around. It's Asher.

"We should go to the train yard tonight. Make a fire, have some booze, and go over that song of yours. I know it isn't finished, but maybe we could help."

I look back into the parking lot and catch a glimpse of Violet. She's approaching some ugly, souped-up Toyota. Leo Wilkins, that lowlife dealer who hangs out by the 76 gas station near the record store, is leaning against the hood. He throws his cigarette to the ground as she approaches the car and motions for her to get in. There's a base meanness in his body language and expression. She does as she's told.

"Earth to Lucien," Asher calls.

"Maybe not the train yard tonight," I say, turning back to him. "But yeah, I think you guys can help. I just need to make a few changes first."

Goetic Prelude in A minor plays over my computer speakers. Each vocal part is a distinct track, played out on the piano and merged together in Pro Tools. Hearing the prelude all together, vibrating through the physical world rather than in my mind, I find myself moved to tears.

The speakers are blaring, the volume pushed to its maximum setting. My desk rumbles with every note deeper than middle C. Despite the cacophony, Mother does not stir from her room.

I take a swig from Father's flask, the last swallow left, then slam it down.

"Amduscias!"

I invoke the name of the demon.

"Come to me, Amduscias. Conductor of the

damned. Grave, Black Unicorn. Sixty-seventh Duke of Hell."

Static overtakes my computer monitor, and in the shifting chaos of black and white dots, the image of a unicorn emerges. It shakes out its mane, casting aside bits of white static stuck in its dark hair.

"Lucien Beaumont. Dark Prince of Enfield and custodian of The Madrigal, *to what do I owe the pleasure?"*

"I don't know what I've done or who I've hurt, but things are going to change."

The monitor dims, and bits of static smoke rise from the unicorn's nostrils.

"Come now, little maestro, you don't get to make the rules. You don't possess the song. The song, dear boy, possess you."

I tremble at the demon's words, afraid they are true, but I take a deep breath and continue. I'm in charge here, no matter what it says.

"No more innocent people will die for this song. No more families who moved into the wrong house. No more troubled composers."

"Great art is not born without sacrifice," Amduscias *says with a snort that cracks the glass of my monitor from the inside.*

I straighten my tie and do my best to seem unafraid. In my mind, I can see the screen cracking in half and Amduscias dragging me back through the monitor and trapping me in the song.

"Sacrifices will still be made, but I will choose them. Criminals and dregs that won't be missed. Men like that junkie my father killed."

"Your father finished just half the measures

because he worked in half-measures. The Madrigal of the World's End *demands full revel in dark pleasures."*

"We play by my rules or we don't play at all, Amduscias. I'll burn the whole fucking score, and there is no backup this time."

Does it know I'm bluffing? I feel that a demon should have a good nose for bullshit, but I hope I'm wrong.

A blast of white noise escapes the speakers, drowning out The Madrigal's *prelude, and Amduscias drags its horn down the inside of the monitor's glass. It cuts like a diamond, and monochrome static drips from inside the monitor and onto my desk.*

"You must, of course, follow your heart. You're the maestro, after all," Amduscias says, drawing back further into the monitor. "And what do I know? I'm just a muse whose soul predates the fall."

The music comes to an abrupt halt, and my speakers squeal with feedback. The screen goes blue, save for an error message about a corrupt data file, bisected by a jagged crack in the glass. The unicorn is gone, and so is the song.

It's Monday night, and the four of us are cruising through Enfield in my mother's car. She made her weekly trip to the liquor store and Family Dollar earlier today, so she won't notice that it's missing.

The car smells like cigarettes, and wine, and a cheap, knockoff version of the perfume Mother used to wear when we still had money. Despite the early autumn chill, it's hot in the car. Four teenage boys crammed in together will do that, especially when one considers Maxwell's exceptional girth and weight. The poor kid is like a walking space heater.

Maxwell is afraid that we'll get pulled over. I suppose the car is technically stolen, and yes, we are drinking, but Asher is driving and at least has a valid license, so it's kind of legal. What we aim to do, however, is not.

Asher and J. C. still want revenge for what the glee club did to us, how they robbed us of the auditorium. I want something different, though. I want to punish a small wretched soul that breathes pain into the world. I want to beat him and bleed him until the missing bars of my song pour out from his wounds. I want to grind the bones of the plebeian swine who would mar a face such as Violet's.

The others can't know that, though. They wouldn't understand, so instead I frame this as a mission of revenge. Violet tried to crush something we love, so we are now crushing something she loves—Leo Wilkins, her abusive, drug-dealing boyfriend.

We're heading toward the 76 gas station over by Jonas's record store, the one where Leo slings dope to middle-schoolers and high school kids. The police never seem to bother him, which I suppose is no surprise. Why would any institution in this day and age do its job? Just another disappointment from those who came before us.

Asher takes a hard left onto Elm Street, and Maxwell spills the bottle of wine we have been passing around. Mother's cream-colored upholstery is instantly stained, and this brings me more joy than anxiety.

"Oh, shit. Watch it, Asher. I'm spilling this all over the car."

Asher laughs and makes a joke about how Maxwell can't hold his liquor. I open the glove box and grab some napkins that I then hand to Maxwell and J. C. in the back seat so that they might wipe up any wine spilled onto their clothes.

We drive two more blocks before taking a right onto Bateman Road. As we turn the corner, I can see the lighted orange sign bearing the number 76. A figure stands beneath the sign, his features hidden by a flat-brimmed baseball cap creeping out from the hood of a sweatshirt. I can't see his face, but I know it's Leo.

"Get your shit together back there, boys," Asher says. "Just another minute till curtain."

We drive past the 76 and park down a nearby side street to avoid the security cameras outside the gas station. I reach under the seat for the stack of four fedoras I placed under there earlier. Each is a genuine felt hat with a wider brim than those stiff, broke-ass hipster knockoffs you find at Target and Walmart. They should conceal our faces from any surveillance lurking above us, without tipping Leo off about our intentions.

Asher puts his on and adjusts it in the rearview, trying to find just the right angle to pull off a sort of ratpack attitude. He smirks, satisfied. I place mine on my head, straight and level.

"Maybe we shouldn't do this, guys," Maxwell calls from the back seat. "I mean, Leo Wilkins is a drug dealer. He might have a gun or something."

"Doubtful," Asher replies. "An illegal gun would land him five years, easy. It's not worth packing in a burb like Enfield, especially when your market is kids."

"Still, we could get in a lot of trouble," Maxwell adds.

"All that pussy you're eating is taking its toll, Maxxy," J. C. says. "You are what you eat, and we know you've got an appetite."

I turn around, my gaze darting between the two of them. Maxwell's cheeks are so red I can see his blushing in the darkness of the car.

"What's he talking about?" I ask.

"I caught Max holding hands with Ashley from the glee club after school today. I wonder what else he's got her holding behind closed doors."

My eyes lock on Maxwell, and my eyebrows rise, silently asking if this is true. *Are you sleeping with the enemy, Maxwell? Are you sullying yourself with the garbage rabble of Swift River High?*

"It just kinda happened. I don't want to make a big deal about it," Maxwell says.

My eyes stay locked with his. His embarrassment morphs into discomfort and finally fear. I turn away. This betrayal . . . no, this indiscretion . . . will have to be dealt with later. Right now we are on a mission.

"Showtime, gentlemen," I say, opening the

147

car door.

We exit the sedan and make our way back on to Bateman road. In my mind's eye, I can see an aerial shot of us strutting down the dark street like film noir gangsters in our suits and fedoras. The camera pans down to show the steel of our expressions and the fire in our eyes. Cue the opening music, something familiar and ironically pleasant— Mozart's *Sonata Facile.*

There are no cars on the road and no pedestrians walking down the street. Enfield goes to bed early on weeknights. The only people who come out this late are the addicts and the jobless nerds ascending from their parents' basements in search of junk food after a long day of video games and pornography. Even those unfortunate souls are absent right now, and a sign taped on the glass door of the station reads *Back in ten,* so we don't even have the clerk to content with. One might call this providence.

As we walk past the gas pumps and toward the façade of the mini-mart attached to the filling station, I can make out Leo's features despite the shadow thrown over his face by his pot leaf baseball cap. He's taking a hit off of his . . . whatever they call those things retards use for vaping . . . and gives us a nod. Even from six yards away I can smell the stench of cheap weed wafting off him.

Asher takes the lead, as is the plan. Leo used to sell him pot, so there is a rudimentary level of trust there, or at least a lack of suspicion.

"I like the threads, my man," Leo says. "Looking sharp. You boys just get back from a funeral or something?"

"Naw," Asher says, with a laugh.

He pulls his right hand out of his pocket. The left is gripping a switchblade in his jacket.

He shakes the dealer's hand, pulls him in close for a one-armed hug. Asher embraces him and buries the knife below the drug dealer's ribs. Not just once but three times in quick succession.

Leo falls, almost in slow motion. His body hits the asphalt, and a gasp escapes his lips. Asher flicks the blood off the knife, and a droplet spins and dances in neon light before it splatters against the ground.

I rush over, delivering a full-on soccer kick to Leo's face. The hard sole of my shoe lacerates his cheek, and a puff of atomized blood sprays from his mouth.

Asher and J. C. join in kicking him. He curls into a ball as we stomp his ribs, face, and legs. Bones snap beneath our heels, and blood pools like oil slicks on the blacktop.

All earlier thoughts of Mozart's pleasant compositions are driven from my mind by the tragic melody of *The Madrigal of the World's End*. Measures I have never heard play in my mind, sung in a language I've never heard. They fill in some of the blanks from the unfinished score. Eighth and sixteenth notes play over the rhythm of our violence. The music flows like a fount.

"Guys, I think that's enough," Maxwell cries, his voice high pitched and wavering.

We don't stop. If anything, our attack grows fiercer. Leo mumbles something, probably a plea for mercy, but I can't hear him over the melodies and counterpoints blaring from the depths of Hell and into my brain. My cup overfloweth with inspiration.

Our kicks play triplets on Leo's huddled form. His hand is crushed beneath Asher's combat boot. The snapping bones sound like the crack of a snare drum. J. C. and I follow, stomping on his torso in a quick succession of bass drum hits.

"Jesus Christ, that's enough!" Maxwell screams. "You're gonna fucking kill him."

Maxwell puts a hand on my shoulder, and he pulls me back. I whip around in anger and glare at him. He backs up a step and stares at me with an expression of fear and sadness.

"Lucien, you need to stop."

"Great art is not born without sacrifice, Maxwell!" I scream, pointing at the battered, blubbering mess that is Leo Wilkins.

"Art? This isn't art, Lucien! This is you throwing your future away . . . throwing your humanity away. And for what? To get even at the goddamn glee club?"

"This is my muse, Maxwell," I say, jabbing my finger toward Leo Wilkins. His baseball cap is dyed crimson, and shreds of skin hang from his face. A deep laceration exposes his shattered cheekbone. Shallow breath produces red foam from his broken nose and past his busted lips.

"Death, and violence, and pain . . . everything that this shithole world has thrown at me . . . at us . . ." I wave my hands, gesturing to the rest of the choir. "I send it back tenfold, and when I do the secrets of *The Madrigal* unfold in my mind."

Maxwell reaches out. His fingertips graze the back of my hand and his lips tremble. Tears well up in his eyes. The others are quiet and still behind me.

"Lucien, this is crazy. We can't . . . I can't do this."

"Then don't."

I turn back to J. C. and Asher, raise my arms as if I'm conducting a symphony, and bring the sole of my Brogue down on Leo's temple. He goes still, but the others, all save Maxwell, join me in kicking him again and again. By the time the flow of music ceases in my head and I direct them to stop, Leo Wilkins is a broken heap of flesh and bone. The only thing recognizable about him is the suburban, drug-dealer chic of his clothing and the stink of marijuana.

The three of us take a minute to catch our breath and adjust our hats and ties. I look around making sure that the clerk hasn't returned from his bathroom break and that no passersby have stumbled upon our crime, and I notice that Maxwell is gone. Poor, kind-hearted, gamma-male Maxwell—despite all his talent and creativity, he just doesn't have the mettle to make the sacrifices that true art demands.

"Where the hell did Max go?" J. C. asks, still catching his breath.

"I think he quit the choir," I answer with more than a little sadness in my voice.

"Lucien, we need to go get him," Asher says in a panicked tone. "What if he goes to the cops?"

"He won't," I say as I start walking back to the car. Asher puts up no further argument, which is good because I have no inclination to bicker. I must capture these new bits of music in paper and ink, and

I don't need the distraction of an argument.

When we get to the car, I retrieve a plastic bag from the trunk and instruct the others to take off their shoes and place them in it. I do the same, then tie it up. We'll throw them away on the ride home, right over the Swift River Bridge, where they'll either sink to the bottom or get carried off to Prescott Lake, a town over. Either way, they'll be lost to any police who might come poking around, along with any bits of Leo Wilkin ground into their soles.

Asher gets back into the driver's seat. I take shotgun, and J. C. stretches out across the back. I grab my songbook from the dashboard and begin writing down the new portions of *The Madrigal* revealed to me through the murder of Leo Wilkins. They let me work in peace, and none of us says a word.

As the car turns back down Bateman Road and past our crime scene, I glance at the side mirror and see the big orange sign for the 76 gas station, but its numbers are backward in the reflection. Below the sign is the still mass we left dead on the asphalt. He gets smaller and smaller, less and less significant the further distance we put between us. I feel no empathy for him. I feel no remorse. Leo was a piece of garbage—a twenty-something-year-old thug who sold dope to children and beat on his high school girlfriend, who was, in truth, light years out of his league.

But enough thinking about Leo. I have a song to transcribe. I need to focus on the things I most want. And my enemies? The people who genuinely want to cause me harm? It's time I leave them in the rearview mirror.

It's nearly midnight, and we sit on the edge of the Swift River, we being J. C., Asher, and myself. We are gathered around the score, so much closer to being finished now. Mother's car is running, and the headlights give us light to study the music by. We pass another bottle of wine back and forth as we review the piece.

"It's not finished yet, but this is enough to get us started," I say. "It's enough to practice and begin learning our parts."

"So is this how you composed the whole thing, like how it came to you while we stomped Leo's ass?" J. C. asks, his eyes scanning the staves on the paper.

"For the most part," I reply. "A little of it was legible in my father's score, the parts my mother failed to destroy. I tried more pedestrian methods to finish the piece, but the spirit of the song only responds to violence."

Asher sings a line, a series of bassy triplets, and howls at the moon when he finishes the bar.

"That melody, Lucien . . . it's powerful. It's intense. Like it could flay the skin right off a person."

"I think it can do that," I tell them, admitting the true nature of the song for the first time. "I think it can drag this whole town down to Hell, with everyone in it."

For the next half hour I tell them the story of *The Madrigal,* as best as I know it. I tell them about

Amduscias, the dreams I've had of Father, the snuff pics I found in my old house that turned into pen and crayon drawings, and of my visits with the late Philip Gravetree.

They don't run, or mock, or even flinch. They smile and howl. We toast with cheap wine, and we sing *The Madrigal of the World's End* into the night. The parts we can, at least. Those no longer consigned to oblivion and Hell.

It's beautiful to hear it come together with real human voices, but something is off. The notes chill my blood and set my synapses aflame with passion, but there is a notable absence that leaves the piece lacking. *The Madrigal of the World's End* is intended for four singers, and we only have three now.

Perhaps Maxwell will come around.

CHAPTER 14

I'm awakened by the smell of gasoline and the sound of bickering. My eyes open, and I find myself staring at the jade linen wallpaper of Philip Gravtree's hall of heroes, complete with the imagery of black unicorns running down gilded deer. When last I was here the creatures were static on the field of green, but now they move across it with a life of their own.

Across from me are portraits—Liszt and Bach. They seem alive in their frames, just like the animals rendered across the wallpaper. The last time I was here they sang to me, and I wonder if they will sing again.

I hear a ruckus from Gravetree's parlor. Two men are arguing, and their voices are unmistakable. Father and Gravetree.

I go to move, to rush toward the parlor, eager to catch even a glimpse of Father, but find that I'm stuck within the wall. My view into Gravetree's home, it seems, is through a window of sorts. I place my hands on the wooden frame of the sash and hoist myself through it.

I fall to the ground and look back at the

opening I had come through. It's clear to me now that it wasn't a window at all but a picture frame. Within the frame, that place that I just crawled out of, is a simple oil painting of the Swift River High auditorium. Asher and J. C. hang from nooses, stretching up past the curtains. A third rope hangs down between them, frayed and severed. Both the noose and the condemned are absent from the rope's end. A brass plate on the frame bears my name, along with the year of my birth, and a second date sixteen years later. I look glance down and realize that I have a slipknot tied around my throat and a tail of burlap rope trailing down my chest like a tie.

"Louis, we need to stop," Gravetree says. His tone has a quality of desperation.

I walk down the hall, toward the parlor. Through the doorway I see them arguing. Father's shirt is unbuttoned, and his tie hangs over his neck like a scarf. His hair is a mess. Black soot stains his face and clothes, and a potpourri of smoke and gasoline wafts off of him. Gravetree is in much the same state, but his wild, white hair is singed, as are the sleeves of his blazer.

"Great art is not born without sacrifice, Philip!" Father screams, pointing at the score that lay atop Gravetree's piano.

"Art? This is no longer art, Louis! This is us throwing our futures away . . . throwing our humanity away. And for what?"

"For The Madrigal, *Phillip!" Father screams. "Our muse makes demands. Death, and violence, and pain . . . everything that this shithole world has thrown at me . . . at us . . ." He reaches out*

and grips Gravetree by the shoulder. "We've sent it back tenfold, and each time we have done so the secrets of The Madrigal *have unfolded in our minds."*

There is such passion in his voice that it hurts my heart. I miss his voice. I miss his intensity. I miss my father.

Gravetree removes Father's hand from his shoulder and holds it between both of his own. His lips tremble and tears well up in his eyes. I'm quiet and still in the hallway.

"Louis, this is madness! We kidnapped a woman and burned her alive, for God's sake! We can't . . . I can't do this anymore."

"Then don't," Father says, pulling his hand away.

He turns away from Gravetree and storms out of the parlor. He walks through me without notice, leaving me to wonder which one of us is the ghost.

I wake up before my alarm, back in my shitty condo bedroom in my shitty senior year of high school. It's still dark but close enough to dawn that I decide to stay awake. I was up late working on *The Madrigal,* so I'm going on four hours of sleep, but I dare not go back to bed. If I were to see Father again in my dreams this morning, I don't think I could bring myself to face the world where he's gone.

Despite having taken a shower last night I take another now, shaking away the dream and anchoring my mind with the pitter-patter rhythm of the water. I sing from *The Madrigal of the World's End,* the vocal part best fitted to my range, savoring the acoustics that the bathroom tiles provide. Mother bangs on the wall, my early morning singing waking her in the next room, but I ignore her, and she soon gives up. She gives up on everything, sooner or later.

I almost wish she would come in screaming at me to quiet down. Imagine her barging in, all piss and vinegar, only to be torn to shreds by the melody echoing off the walls. That would be a sight to see— her feeble body collapsing, blood seeping from her eyes and ears. Her bones shattering beneath skin flayed by sound waves. To see her reduced to nothing, to see her erased, the way she tried to erase Father's legacy by destroying the score. I would like that very much, but it doesn't happen. She can't be bothered.

I shut off the water, towel myself dry, and stare in the mirror. I don't like mirrors very much. The thing looking back at me isn't regal. It is a fallen prince, with shaggy hair and black circles around its eyes. It's an angry revenant—a ghost of nobility.

On the back of the toilet is a cheap candle, set in thick glass. I grasp it and bludgeon the mirror. The candle holds, but the mirror shatters. Instead of relieving me of my reflection, I'm met with a dozen versions of my own face looking back at me, each smaller and more pathetic than the large one had been. They are not even complete images but shards of a broken boy, barely held together within a cheap frame.

I leave the bathroom in disgust and go to my

room, where I lay out one of my favorite suits, my finest French-cut shirt and a slim silk tie, the color of absolute darkness. With each piece of clothing I put on, a bit of my self-loathing fades. As I button up my shirt, my shame at living in this tiny condo, encroached upon by Mother's filth and nihilism, recedes. My embarrassment at having to walk the halls amongst the adolescent animals of Swift River High diminishes as I align my belt buckle with the centerline of my shirt and slacks. The feeling of smallness that comes with the gravity of living in a tiny, black-hole town all but vanishes as I set my tie into a Windsor and the cufflinks into my sleeves.

There is an old adage that clothes make the man, though most shun traditional wisdom these days. I can attest that it's true, though. A great many old ideas have value that the masses are blind to. The postmodern man is unwilling to embrace anything of true value because to do so takes effort. From music to fashion to philosophy, everything in this age speaks of disposability, convenience, and ease.

In such a world, the simple act of wearing a suit and tie can set a man a world above, both in aesthetic and character. Despite the crumbling of the Beaumont house, despite having fallen from the arms of wealth and love to the viper pit of my mother's many failures, I still hold myself to the standards of civility.

I put on my jacket, securing only the top button, and leave the house. It's cold outside, in the predawn hours, and my breath floats on the air. Brittle, amber leaves crunch underfoot as I stroll listlessly. No one else is out, save for the occasional early-morning commuter trying to beat the rush into Boston or Cambridge, and I feel alone in the world. Not the kind of inner desolation that besets me when at home or in a crowd but the peaceful detachment of Thoreau.

For the better part of an hour, I weave between side streets and back roads, taking a circuitous path to school as the sun peaks above the horizon. I turn down the corner of a tiny one-way with pickup trucks parked in nearly every driveway, and what do I see? My dear Maxwell, dressed in a T-shirt the size of a tarp and formless denim jeans—the same kind of plebeian garb he wore before we were friends. He's walking the doughy glee club girl named Ashley down the brick walkway of an aging Victorian home, presumably hers. Hand in hand, they both trot in a goofy, graceless manner.

The first notes of *The Madrigal* float off my lips in the form of a whistle. Maxwell looks back, now noticing me. His skin turns white. Ashley waves at me and smiles, which means he hasn't told her about last night and what we did to Leo Wilkins. I wave back, more for his benefit than hers. I take a kind of petty joy in seeing the fear in his eyes, even though I wish him no harm.

"Tie them up and make them sing with knife or rusted spoon. Tie them up and make them sing, and I'll control the tune."

"No," I mutter to Amduscias, who whispers straight into my mind.

Maxwell ushers Ashley forward, ignoring my presence and perhaps trying to put some distance between us. There's no need for that, though. The distance is already there.

"Your individual parts, gentleman. At least what we have so far."

I hand photocopies of the score for *The Madrigal of the World's End* across the lunch table to Asher and J. C. The song is still incomplete, and there are more notes revealed than words, but it's enough to get us started.

Their respective parts are marked with yellow highlighter. Both of them grin, flipping through the pages. J. C. hums the notes of the second tenor part, and Asher bobs his head while reviewing the Baritone stave.

"What the fuck language is this?" J. C. asks.

"An old one." It's the only answer I can give.

"Are you still down to add some percussion?" Asher asks.

Before I can answer, Ari Cole walks by and makes a snide comment. Something about how pathetic it is that even Maxwell, whom he calls fat boy, is too cool to hang out with us now. We all ignore Ari, even though his putrid cologne lingers in a cloud behind him, and instead look over to Maxwell. He sits on the outer edge of the glee club table, where Violet is conspicuously absent. His new girlfriend is resting her head on his shoulder, more at ease than he is. I can see him tense as we glare at him. His face reddens as he willfully ignores us.

"Yes. Let's add some percussion," I say. It's not the rat-a-tat-tat of a snare drum that comes to mind, though. It's something else.

Asher begins humming along with J. C. and taps out a beat on the table. It's primal and brutal but, juxtaposed with the melodies that the two of them hum, it strikes a balance between savagery and class. It holds a unique kind of beauty. A kind of magic.

"Well, the song isn't finished, so who's next?" J. C. asks. "Where will maestro find his muse?"

Asher nods in the direction of the glee club table.

"They're singers. Imagine what secret music their screams could reveal," Asher suggests.

It's unclear if he means Maxwell and Ashley or the glee club kids as a whole, but my skin erupts into goosebumps at the suggestion. His words remind me of what Amduscias proposed this morning. *Tie them up and make them sing with knife or rusted spoon. Tie them up and make them sing, and I'll control the tune.*

Is the demon whispering to the others now, planting ideas in their minds? Is it angry that I've taken control of our relationship?

It doesn't matter. Let Amduscias do its worst. *The Madrigal* is mine now, and I will compose it as I see fit. Sacrifices must still be made, of course, but I will be the one who determines the nature of those offerings.

I scan the lunchroom for another sacrifice, one of my own choosing. Across the cafeteria Ari Cole is holding a freshman in a headlock, forcing the poor bastard's face into his sweaty, post-gym-class armpit.

"They'll get theirs," I say, dismissing the glee

club as a target, eager to assert my dominance over the black unicorn. Eager to shut down its manipulations. "I have another person in mind. Someone who needs a lesson in art appreciation."

CHAPTER 15

It's Wednesday afternoon, and I've decided to kill Ari Cole. I'm not sure yet how or when, but I know that I will. The problem is, of course, that we all have motive, and we would be caught. All it would take is one of those big-mouth pieces of garbage at school to tell the cops about him pissing on my suit, and the law would be all over me. If we got caught, I would never reveal the rest of *The Madrigal,* and we would never have the opportunity to perform it. That's simply unacceptable, so I mull it over as I sort out a new shipment of records at work.

I'm alone, aside from the company of Paganini. Through the proxy of some concert violinist, he plays out his twenty-four caprices while I work. I could not ask for better company. Maxwell can have his stupid, fat girlfriend.

I wish I was putting away records of intrinsic value. Instead, I'm sorting through disposable pop, rock, and hip-hop albums, all vying for attention like musical peacocks with their gauche, technicolor covers or dreary art-school photography. Perhaps if they put more thought into their music, these so-called artists would not have to rely on imagery so steeped in the ostentatious and vulgar. Real music does not require the visual accompaniment of overflowing cleavage, stacks of cash, or cartoonish, neon artwork.

The entryway bell rings behind me, pulling me from my reverie. I turn and see Violet Sarkissian crossing the threshold of the shop. She's dressed in all black, from her skin-tight yoga pants to her baggy Swift River High School sweatshirt. She storms in and whips off her sunglasses, revealing the yellowish bruise around her eye, and marches right up to me.

She's furious. That much is clear. There is a sexiness to her rage. It burns behind her eyes, setting them aglow.

"Did you and your little freak squad jump Leo Wilkins last night?"

I regard her coolly, then go back to straightening the stack of records in front of me.

"Isn't that the scumbag who sells Vicodin to eighth graders in front of the 76?"

She grabs my shoulder and spins me around, so she can look me in the eye. Her face is so close I can feel her breath. I inhale, letting it fill my lungs.

"Don't bullshit me, you fucking weirdo," she says, grabbing my tie and pulling me forward. I find myself wanting to kiss her. "The cops have video of a bunch of assholes in suits and ties kicking the shit out of him?"

I reach up and run my fingers along her jawline.

"Maybe he pissed off the wrong people. What's it to you, prom queen?"

She tightens her grip on my tie and pulls me to her, the anger in her eyes transforming into lust.

"You know damn well we have a thing," she says. "Did you do this because of me? To get back at me for ratting out your creepy virgin choir?"

I did it for you, Violet. Because I love and hate everything about you, and the thought of some common dope slinger putting his hands on you cuts my heart open.

"I was composing a piece of music last night," I say, holding her watery gaze. "I do hope he wasn't hurt too bad, though."

Our lips touch, then part for our tongues to mingle. She tastes like cherries and aged whiskey.

"Lucien," she says, no longer able to hold back her tears, "this isn't a fucking game. Leo's in a coma. He might die, and he didn't do a damn thing to you."

Did she say Leo *might* die? Meaning he's still alive? But why would Amduscias stop the music before we killed him? And why would the demon reveal so much of the song without a proper sacrifice?

Violet lets go of my tie and takes a step back. Her face is a mask of fear and loathing, and I worry that my own expression has betrayed me.

"Oh my God. You thought he was dead. You meant to kill him."

Her words are just above a whisper, nearly lost below the violin playing over the speakers.

"Maybe whoever did this . . . maybe they see more value in you than you realize. Maybe they couldn't stand the thought of some shitbag dope slinger putting their hands on you," I say, reaching up and running my fingers, ever so gently, across her black eye.

"Maybe they did this *for* you, and not *because* of you."

She knocks my hand away and stumbles backward. The music stops, as the last caprice on this side of the record comes to an end, leaving us in silence. Her full, pink lips tremble. I find her terror as arousing as I do her anger.

"You stay the hell away from me!" she screams, then turns and runs.

Even overcome with emotion as she is, her natural grace comes through as she flees. There is a rhythm and cadence to her movement. I find myself speculating that she may have taken ballet at some point. I'm sure of it, in fact. More secret virtue she hides from this vampire of a world.

The bell rings again as the door closes behind her, and I'm left in silence. I detest silences, so I walk over to the turntable and flip the record to side B. After a few moments of soft, scratchy static, the sound of the thirteenth caprice fills the air.

I let Asher and J. C. know that Leo Wilkins is alive but in a coma. They're panicked. Asher wants to sneak into the hospital and put something in his IV to finish the job, but it's not worth the risk. If Leo wakes up, he won't rat us out. He's too much of an idiot hood rat to go to the police. If he survives, he'll come to us, looking for some bullshit hip-hop street justice, and we'll be waiting.

My concern is that we were set up . . . or at least I was set up. Amduscias and its infernal choir sang new parts of *The Madrigal* in my mind as we kicked the snot out of Leo, but the music didn't stop because we let up. It left off at a natural cadence. A section of the song came to its end. But why would Amduscias give me that much if we hadn't finished Leo off? I got less from murdering Gravetree. Did the demon want us to get caught? I intend to find out.

I go to take a swig from my flask but find it empty. A bottle of Bombay Sapphire is overturned on the floor, just as dry.

Fuck it.

My fingers dance across the keys of my piano, playing the bass and countertenor parts to the first movement of *The Madrigal, Black Unicorn Sonata*. Like a musical King Solomon, I invoke the name Amduscias, the infernal conductor and sixty-seventh duke of Hell.

The sharps and flats of my keyboard evaporate into obsidian mist and congeal into a dismembered equine head. Tendrils of jet smoke spiral from its gaseous mane and take the form of a dark horn. Brackish, diseased condensation drips from its chin to form a beard.

"Good evening, Master Beaumont. To what do I owe the pleasure of this summons?"

"You knew Wilkins wasn't dead. You gave me so much of the song, but the sacrifice wasn't complete. Why?"

I continue playing, even though the black keys have dissolved. My fingers still reach for the sharps and flats, and the proper sounds are produced despite their absence on the keyboard. There's no feeling of resistance below my fingers when I hit the space of the missing keys but rather the vacuous pull of a microcosmic singularity.

"As you pointed out, O maestro and great exorcist, we play by your rules now, or The Madrigal *will not exist."*

"Bullshit. You wanted us to think he was dead. You're pissed that I won't be your puppet, so you showed me the song before we killed him, all so we'd have to look over our shoulders if he wakes up."

"Maestro made the choice to cease the beating. Maestro chose to stop the invocation of bleeding. As you pointed out, I am but a muse. When you're the match, I am the fire. When you're the flint, I am the fuse."

I close my eyes and think of my father. Did he sit at his own piano, playing these same bars, having this same circular discussion with the spirit of the song? Did Amduscias play him, the way it is trying with me? Or did Father have a tighter grip than I?

When I open my eyes, the black keys have returned to my piano. The vision of Amduscias has vanished and its mocking voice has gone silent, but I still feel the demon's presence.

I tell myself I'm still in control. I tell myself that *The Madrigal* is mine to compose. I don't believe it, though.

CHAPTER 16

Ms. Kane is silent as she studies me from across her desk. She's looking for something in my eyes or maybe in my expression. Hunting for something.

"Is everything okay, Ms. Kane?"

She doesn't answer right away. Instead, her gaze intensifies, scrutinizing my expression and body language.

"Is it, Lucien?" she finally asks. "Is there anything you want to tell me? Maybe about some trouble you've gotten into?"

Someone has told her about Leo Wilkins. Maybe it was Violet. Maybe Maxwell. Hell, it could have been the police, for all I know. Someone's been talking, though, and that's bad whatever way you slice it.

"Not that I can think of," I say, trying my best to keep an even tone.

She frowns and makes a brief note on her legal pad.

"Lucien, I can't help you unless you open up to me. Did something bad happen the other night?"

In my head I can hear the bits of *The*

Madrigal that played out as we beat Leo Wilkins into a coma. I can almost feel his bones give way beneath my feet. My nostrils fill with the smell of his blood and the skunkweed scent of his clothes.

"Nothing bad at all," I say, with complete honesty. Well, almost complete. I suppose Wilkins surviving isn't so great. Also, there is the matter of Maxwell's defection.

"I see," she replies and marks down another note. Her tax-dollar driven, prostitute smile is absent today.

"Lucien, you're a smart, creative kid, but you're angry. Angrier than I think I realized. God knows you have reason to be pissed at the world. You miss your dad. Your mother has retreated into herself. You've lost wealth and status. You don't fit in."

I laugh, not with bitterness or sarcasm. It's a genuine laugh that almost feels good.

"Is this supposed to make me feel better?" I ask.

She stares into my eyes, all business. My momentary sense of relief fades.

"Smart and angry is a bad combination."

Words, paragraphs worth, detach themselves from Ms. Kane's legal pad. They stretch and spin into tendrils of ink, writhing above her.

"It pushes you to internalize and write off the rest of the world as stupid or useless."

The dark tendrils meet and congeal.

"It makes you want to flaunt what you perceive as your own superiority, maybe at first by dressing better than everyone, but maybe later you start hurting people."

A disembodied unicorn head forms from ink and floats in the air.

"People who are cruel to you? People who are less gifted but have the things you want?"

"She's got you made now, maestro. She knows all about you," Amduscias says, with an expression as close to arrogance as its inky, equine features can manage. "She's got you made now, maestro. You know what you must do."

I steeple my fingers to keep my hands from trembling and lean back. I don't want either Ms. Kane or Amduscias to see how nervous I am.

"I assure you, I'm in control," I say to both the demon and the counselor.

Amduscias lets out an arrogant huff of annoyance. Smoke, the color of pitch, erupts from its snout.

Ms. Kane caps her pen and frowns. She's silent for a moment. I wait for her to tell me that my choir was identified assaulting Wilkins and that the cops are waiting outside the room. She doesn't, though.

"You should go back to class, Lucien. I don't think we'll be meeting anymore."

Her statement sends a cold shudder down my spine, and Amduscias is gone from the room. It's as if her words held the power of some ancient exorcism. My mouth hangs open dumbly.

"Why not?" I ask, unsure why the thought bothers me. I should be relieved, happy even. But I'm not.

"If you aren't going to tell me the truth, then

this isn't going to work. It's a waste of your time and mine."

I nod and rise to my feet. An odd series of non-sequitur images flash through my mind. Father's corpse swinging from a noose. Mother drunk and passed out. Larson seeing me off on my last day at the Academy. Maxwell walking hand in hand with Ashley.

I proceed to the door, and as I touch the knob Ms. Kane calls out my name. I turn to look at her, hoping for something but unsure what.

"There's more to life than this town," she says. "Don't lose sight of that."

"We need to talk," I say, sitting down at the lunch table and interrupting a conversation J. C. and Asher are having about music theory and syncopation. "I think Ms. Kane knows about the other night."

They stare at me, the gravity of my words taking a moment to set in. Confusion turns to anxiety on J. C.'s face and anger on Asher's. A plastic knife vibrates in J. C.'s trembling hand.

"How?" he asks in a whisper.

"No clue." I shake my head. "I'm not sure what she knows exactly or how she knows it. She kept asking if I was in trouble and insinuated that maybe I had hurt some people."

Asher glares across the cafeteria, over at the glee club table. Maxwell is sitting next to his new girlfriend, laughing with our enemies. Violet is eating quietly, hidden behind her sunglasses and beneath her hood. Every few seconds her eyes dart to her cell phone. Smart money says she's waiting for some life-or-death news regarding Leo Wilkins.

"It was one of them," Asher growls. "Max or Violet. Maybe both."

J. C. looks as if he's about to hyperventilate, and his face is beet red. Repeated, whispered profanities dribble from his mouth. I tell him to get a handle on himself.

"What are we gonna do, Lucien?" he asks, on the verge of panic.

"First thing we need to do is make sure Wilkins doesn't wake up," Asher suggests. "Then we take care of those two."

Maxwell glances over, sees us staring, and turns his head in the other direction so fast I'm surprised he doesn't get whiplash. He's scared. Maybe he did rat us out.

"It's too risky to go after Wilkins in a hospital full of people. There's a good chance he's not going to make it anyway."

"We don't know that," J. C. says, his voice cracking.

Asher leans back and stretches his arms up high. He cracks his knuckles above his head and lets out a long breath.

"Lucien's right. Wilkins can't say shit, for now at least, and Violet is grasping at straws. We should deal with the immediate threat."

I look back over to Maxwell and his goofy, fat girlfriend. He's smiling and laughing, and as pissed as I am at him for walking away, I can't help but be a little happy for him. Even after the other night, he's one of the few people in this world I don't want to bleed like a pig.

"We don't know that Maxwell blabbed," I say.

"Lucien, come on, man," Asher says, shaking his head. "I know you're half-gay for fat boy, but someone's been talking."

He's right, of course. Ms. Kane wouldn't have blown me off if she didn't think she had a good reason, something more substantial than grainy surveillance footage or Violet Sarkissian's suspicions. It had to be Maxwell. And if he told her, what's keeping him from talking to the police?

"Let me talk to him."

"For fuck's sake, Lucien," J. C. gasps.

"Just let me talk to him. I can pull him back in. We still need a countertenor for *The Madrigal*."

They grumble as I get up. I turn to cross the cafeteria, and Asher shouts that I'm wasting my time. I pray that he's wrong.

With each step I take toward Maxwell the temperature drops and the coldness between us takes on physical form. My icy breath hangs in the air, taking the form of tiny damned souls. They sing The Madrigal, *urging me to violence in its name.*

Is this how things were between Debussy and Ravel after their split? Were they consumed by anger and cold? Did Wagner hear demonic whisperings, urging him to hurt Nietzsche after the philosopher betrayed him and set fire to their friendship?

I close my eyes and try to banish the hateful spirits inhabiting that cold space between Maxwell and myself. When I open them the world is mundane once more. Unhaunted, at least for the moment, I walk over to Maxwell's seat. His new glee club friends greet me with sarcasm and ice-cold stares. That's fine. I'm not here to talk to them.

"Maxwell, may I have a moment?"

"Lucien, please just go away."

He doesn't even bother to turn and look at me as he speaks.

"This is important," I insist.

"Hey, Brooks Brothers, the kid doesn't want to be in your freaky-deaky club anymore," says the kid I know only as Karaoke Joe.

"This is a Gucci, thank you very much," I retort. "Not that I'd expect you to know the difference."

While I'm distracted a mass of gravy-drenched mashed potatoes strikes my shoulder. All the tables around me erupt into laughter, though Maxwell continues staring straight forward, afraid to meet my gaze.

I scan the cafeteria and see Ari Cole cracking up as one of his mongoloid jock friends holds a potato-encrusted spoon in the air and soaks up the praise for humiliating me.

I'm already turning toward the jock table, a hundred violent responses dancing in my head, when a fat red apple strikes the jock in the eye like a fastball. He falls over, clutching his face, and a few people make vulgar exclamations.

"How do you like them apples, fuckface?" Asher yells from our table, holding his arms out like a dying Christ. I smile. It feels good to know that someone has my back, even if Maxwell doesn't.

Ari Cole leans over to check on his friend, who's hunched into a ball, then he stands up and whips a carton of chocolate milk back at Asher. With those volleys fired, the lunchroom descends into utter madness. Food and trash fly from every table, in every direction. Teachers scream for order, their demands lost beneath the howling of a hundred teenagers.

I turn back to Maxwell, hoping I can usher him away in the chaos, so we might have a word, but he's gone. Looking around, I see him halfway across the cafeteria, fleeing and shielding his girlfriend from culinary debris with his jacket.

"Maxwell!" I scream, trying to project above the cacophony of the food fight.

He turns for a moment, and I can read enough fear and guilt in his expression to answer my question. Maxwell did rat us out. Definitely to Ms. Kane, if not to the cops. And even if he hasn't gone to the police yet, he will soon. J. C. and Asher are right. It breaks my heart, but this must be dealt with.

CHAPTER 17

I wake up in my bedroom, not the one in the tiny condo but my room in the house on Raylene Street. It's four years before I will meet Maxwell, Asher, or J. C. Four years before I will fall in love and hate with Violet Sarkissian. But it's only minutes before Father kills himself. It's too dark to see the calendar on my wall, and the green number display of my alarm clock blinks a nonsensical zero-sixty-seven, but I know when I am.

From the other room I hear music, mad and off-putting. The composition is strange, played in an odd meter. Bars begin with strong resolve and decline in tension with each passing note. Accents fall on the second beat instead of the third. Its rhythm is disjointed and its harmony erratic, almost as if it's being played backward.

I cast aside my blankets and step out of bed. The floor is cool beneath my feet from the winter chill leaching through our old sash windows. I walk toward my bedroom door, a black rectangle surrounded by a thin border of gleaming light.

My hand falls upon the cold brass knob, and an anemic screech issues from the latch. Soft, warm *light pours in as I open the door. It warms me and banishes the darkness, and I almost convince myself this isn't a nightmare.*

My footfalls are silent beneath the increasing cacophony of the song echoing down the hall. I can see the soundwaves ripple through the air. Concentric circles, like those that radiate out from a rock dropped into a pond. Everything they touch is met with unchecked entropy. Paint peels and crumbles, revealing rotten wood writhing with termites and larvae beneath. Brass hinges tarnish before my eyes, and doorknobs turn the odd green of aged patina. Floorboards warp and crack, lacerating my bare feet with splinters and rusty, protruding nails.

Only I seem unharmed by the sound. It could be that it only ravages inanimate objects, but my dream logic tells me that isn't so. The song can't hurt me, because I'm special. That's the only reason I'm safe, and I know it. But I also know a contradictory truth, just as real, as contradictions often are in dreams, that I'm safe because the song is contained, and I'm not hearing it right. Someone is protecting me from it.

I know that both things are true, just as I know that neither are.

I reach for the patinated doorknob, and the music stops. The sound ends so abruptly, and the world around me goes so quiet, that I find myself doubting any music ever played.

The door is locked, and the knob refuses to move other than a wiggle. From the other side, Father's voice breaks the silence.

CURTIS M. LAWSON

"You can't have them!" he yells in a choked cry. "I'm done with this! Done with you!"

I rattle the door, calling out to Father. I scream for him as tears well in my eyes.

"You are no King Solomon, Louis Beaumont, nay. Not even an Erich Zann, I would say," Amduscias retorts inside Father's office. "You are weak, and I am strong. You lack the power to bind me in circle or song."

My fists slam against the dry, dead wood of the door. Splinters bite into my hands, but the door doesn't give.

"Philip was right—this song is a curse!" Father screams.

"If you'll not give your son to the song, O great exorcist and maestro, I'll give the song to your son and let the young Beaumont have a go," Amduscias replies.

A glass bottle clatters on the other side of the door, and I hear something being wheeled across the floor.

"No," Father resolves. "The Madrigal dies with me."

A loud bang, like something heavy falling over, issues from Father's office. A choked gurgling follows, juxtaposed against musical laughter.

I kick and punch the door, over and over. Finally it opens. Some conscious part of me screams at my younger self not to look. It screams for me to avert my gaze. I don't listen, and my punishment for disobedience is the visage of my father swinging from a noose above his overturned desk chair. His eyes are bulging, and his complexion has turned an ugly purple.

I scream for Mother to come help. I call for her to come save Father, the way he saved her when she overdosed. I scream and beg for her to save our family. She doesn't, though. She doesn't answer at all.

Pages of sheet music swirl like a dust devil around Father's dying form. Wet, shiny ink blacks out the staves.

Amduscias appears beside me, but with a sort of dream logic I realize the demon has been there all along. The unicorn's snout nuzzles my cheek, and its beard tickles my shoulder as it whispers to me.

"Look upon your father, and let your heart turn to black ice. Today you learn great art is not born without sacrifice."

My pillow is saturated with tears when I wake up. The backward rendition of *The Madrigal* echoes in my ears as I shake the nightmare fog from my mind.

It was just a bad dream, I tell myself, knowing damn well that isn't the truth. Yes, it was framed within the acid-trip logic of a lucid nightmare, but those things really happened. Father killed himself in that office, and I found him there. Someone blacked out his score of *The Madrigal,* and maybe it was Father himself rather than Mother. Maybe he hated and feared the song as much as Gravetree had. Maybe when Gravetree played it backward it sounded familiar to me because Father had done the same, in some vain attempt to seal Amduscias within the song, like a musical exorcism.

Had Amduscias demanded Father kill me for the song? Did the monster hold back the last bits of music from him, demanding some horrid, Abrahamic sacrifice?

Great art is not born without sacrifice.

The thought hits me like a wrecking ball to the gut, forcing me to choke back the rising bile in my throat. It's too much to think about: that Father died to save me from Amduscias. The idea that *The Madrigal* isn't his legacy but a curse that drove him into the noose—my head spins just considering it.

Great art is not born without sacrifice.

I get up and go about my morning routine, unsure what else to do. I put on some music, *Nuvole Bianche* by Ludovico Einaudi, hoping that the melancholy piano will drive the piecemeal music of *The Madrigal of the World's End* from my brain. I lay out my clothes and accessories across my bed, intentionally losing myself in any song but the one I've been obsessing over. I shower and dress, keeping music playing the whole time—all piano sonatas and concertos. Nothing of a choral nature that might remind me of Amduscias. Nothing that might remind me of *The Madrigal of the World's End.*

Once I'm dressed, I move to the kitchen where I pour myself a bowl of raisin bran and a cup of Earl Grey with a shot of whatever booze is closest to the tea kettle. I close my eyes and focus on the music. I let it exorcize the remnants of my nightmare and remove me from this shitty little condo and this shitty little town. I let it carry me back in time to the days I sat on Father's lap, playing simple songs on the baby grand in his office.

With breakfast done, I decide I won't go to school today. Instead, I sit at my little out-of-tune piano, and I play. Not the music of Hell but the music of legends. *Für Elise* and *Ode to Joy. Nocturne No. 2 in E Flat major.* Sitting there, playing the songs of the masters, reminds me of the summer with Maxwell, and our easy friendship before school started. Before I found *The Madrigal.* Before Violet Sarkissian and Ari Cole. Before J. C. and Asher and The Black Heart Boys' Choir.

I don't want to kill Maxwell. I don't want to sacrifice him to Amduscias, as Father was supposed to do to me. I know, however, that he'll go to the police if we don't. Maybe he already has. What else is there to do?

I could just run—forget about *The Madrigal* and this black-hole town. I could leave today. Pack up a few suits, empty Mother's accounts, and take a bus to New York, all before Maxwell gets us arrested. Before someone connects me to the murdered family on Raylene Street or to the late Philip Gravetree.

That was the plan when I first left the Academy, right? That was the plan before I got distracted and obsessed with this cursed song. Finish school and get the hell out of Enfield. It's as Ms. Kane said, there's more to life than this town.

"You wouldn't leave this unfinished, Master Beaumont," Amduscias says from the depths of Hell and into my psyche and soul. *"Not when we're so*

deep in love."

"Watch me," I say aloud, standing up from my piano bench. I grab my copy of *The Madrigal,* the object of my obsession, and I take it to the kitchen. I light the stove, ready to burn it as Gravetree did, but I hesitate. The music plays through my head, more beautiful and majestic than anything in all creation.

"You wouldn't leave this unfinished, Master Beaumont. Art trumps all, when push comes to shove."

"You took my father, you son of a bitch, but you won't take Maxwell, and you won't take me."

Amduscias responds with a knowing laughter, rather than a rhyming taunt.

My phone vibrates in my pocket. I retrieve it and see Asher's name on the display. I answer, afraid that I already know what he has to say.

"Hello."

"We've got him. Figured we could sing one last song together and see if you can finish *The Madrigal*. Meet us at the practice space."

The line goes dead. My stomach flips, and my blood runs cold. *I stare into the rising flames of my gas range, and in the fire I see a laughing unicorn.*

It's just past nine in the morning when I get to the overgrown train tracks leading to the old railway station. It's cold out, the coldest it's been all fall, and the rusted rails lie hidden beneath a blanket of amber and burgundy leaves. The scent of the dirt, the trees, and the air is different, even from how it smelled a few weeks ago. The earthy, living smells of summer have all faded, leaving the scent of decay and oncoming winter in their wake.

Dead foliage rustles as I walk beneath the arched boughs of ancient trees that come together with such symmetry that it leaves no doubt in my mind this world has an architect, cruel as that intelligence may be. Maxwell and I often noted over the summer that passing through this natural gateway felt like leaving the real world behind. Today doesn't feel like that, though. The black-hole gravity of Enfield still pulls at me as I tread beneath the trees, perhaps even more than usual.

The last time I came here I found a measure of happiness sharing this secret, forgotten place with Maxwell, Asher, and J. C. Our choir was of one mind, united in our hatred for the tepid souls of this town, and in our love of music. We sang, and drank, and laughed. Now I follow the tracks with a sick feeling in my gut, dreading what I'll find at their end.

The pathway of trees opens into a clearing, and there in its center is the dilapidated Enfield railway station. This place was once beautiful to me—these secret, wondrous ruins. Today I see it as a graveyard. Rusted corpses of boxcars and ancient engines sit beside the crumbling, rotted façade of the train platform. The painted mural of the Boston and Albany Railroad Company's logo on the platform wall is faded and barely legible, like the markings of a weathered gravestone. I fear that more than dead locomotives and forgotten history will be buried here by the day's end.

As I get closer, I can hear Maxwell crying and blubbering from inside a derelict boxcar. I take a deep breath and straighten my tie. It's important to maintain my composure, whatever I walk into. The situation may still be salvageable, regardless of what Maxwell has said about us or what J. C. and Asher may have done to him. There's a chance I can still fix this.

My heart races as I close the final yards to the train. Maxwell's voice gets louder with each step, but his words are unintelligible babble, broken up by deep sobs. Bitter, acidic bile fills my throat and pollutes my mouth. I swallow it back, then take a swig of gin from my flask.

The door to the boxcar is missing, having long ago fallen off and oxidized into brittle rust and orange dust. I can't see inside from my vantage point, but I can hear my fractured choir inside—Maxwell crying while J. C. and Asher mock him.

I boost myself up into the car, mindful not to catch my clothes or flesh on any jagged bits of rusty metal or splintered wood. Decades-old grime soils my hands and my suit, but sometimes you can't avoid getting dirty.

What I find inside, once I'm on my feet, is worse than I could have imagined. There on the floor, bloody and naked, is Ashley, Maxwell's tubby glee club girlfriend. She's on her side, with her hands ziptied together behind her back. Chunks of her hair are missing, and her face is a bruised, swollen mess. They've carved the word *PIG* into her chest and stuffed her mouth with a rotten crabapple. I stare at her, waiting for her chest to rise and fall. After the better part of a minute goes by, I realize that breathing just isn't something she does anymore.

"Top o' the morning, maestro," J. C. says in a jovial, faux Irish accent.

At the far end of the car, Maxwell is bound to a decrepit wooden chair, a relic of the train yard. Zipties cut into his wrists and ankles, lashing him to the armrests and the front legs of the chair. A big, wet piss spot stains his baggy sweatpants. There are at least six or seven cuts and burns decorating his cheeks and forehead. His T-shirt is pulled up past his massive belly, exposing a half-dozen more lacerations. Each is only an inch or two long, but they are bleeding profusely, and the majority of his exposed flesh is painted crimson.

I can still fix this, I say in my head, knowing damn well it's a lie.

Asher stands in front of Maxwell, smoking a fat cigar and tapping out a beat on his captive's head with a pair of drumsticks. J. C. leans against the wall of the boxcar, twirling a butterfly knife and tilting back a bottle of Sam Adams.

Maxwell looks over at me with pleading, watery eyes.

"Lucien, don't let them do this," he begs.

Asher twirls one of the drumsticks and smacks Maxwell in the forehead with the fat end, right on one of his cuts. It makes a dull thud noise that carries through the boxcar.

"You did this to yourself, Maxxy, when you went around blabbing about Wilkins."

I step around the corpse of Ashley from glee club, Ashley who will never again butcher a Disney song or hold hands with poor Maxwell. I walk over to my friend and kneel down, so I can look into his eyes. He cries with shameless abandon, the tears leaving streaks in the blood on his face.

"How did things come to this?" I whisper, more to myself than to anyone else.

"Lucien, please . . ."

"I heard his bitch telling one of the other glee club losers that she and Max have been jogging here in the morning, trying to lose some that whale blubber. We got here first."

I stand up and turn to J. C. My eyes meet his, then Asher's. I make no attempt to hide my anger.

"Why didn't you loop me in on this? Why would you do this without me?"

"Would you have gone along with it if we told you, Lucien?" Asher asks. We all know the answer, so I don't say anything.

"He's your friend, man, I get it. I'm not calling you out, but it had to be done, so we did it."

I turn my back on everyone and run my hand through my hair—hair that has grown all too long and unkempt. I mumble curses under my breath and fight to keep my breakfast in my stomach.

"Maxwell," I say without turning to face him, "tell me you kept your mouth shut, and maybe we can still fix this."

I turn back around and kneel in front of him again. My heart breaks at the sight of his blood-streaked face. "Tell me you're still one of us, and this was all a misunderstanding."

He doesn't need to answer. The trembling of his lip and the squinting of his eyes tell me all I need to know. He ratted us out, and not just to Ms. Kane.

"You went to the cops?" I ask, standing up and taking a step back.

"We got that much out of him already," Asher says.

I suppose I knew already that he'd turned on us. It was clear that he'd talked to Ms. Kane about what we did to Leo Wilkins, but to think that he would go to the police . . . to think that he would betray me so completely . . . that hurt more than anything Ari Cole, or Violet Sarkissian, or even Mother could throw at me.

"You would send me to prison, Maxwell? You'd outright betray me?"

"Please don't kill me. Fuck, Lucien. I don't wanna die."

"I want to hear you say it. Did you betray me to the fucking police?"

"What the hell was I supposed to do?" he screams. "You guys almost fucking killed Leo Wilkins, Lucien! I wasn't going to jail for that."

My fingers ball into a fist, and I gnash my teeth. Without thinking, I punch Maxwell so hard that his head bounces off the back of the chair.

"You fucked it all up, Maxwell." I punch him again, this time with my other fist. "I told Amduscias he couldn't have you, and look what you've done."

He stares at me with a bovine dumbness. He stares at me as if I'm mad.

"The choir needed you!" I scream "*The Madrigal* needed you!"

I grab him by the hair with both hands and bring my face close to his. The tips of our noses touch, and I can feel his warm, wet blood. I stare into his eyes and realize we are both crying now.

"I needed you." This time my words are a whisper, and they are the last words I have for him.

I kiss his lips, then turn away. Behind me, he begs and pleads. I ignore him and take a sip from my flask, savoring the taste of juniper. I put the gin away, then take off my tie. The silk feels good on my hands as I wrap one side around each fist. It makes a satisfying snap when I tug it tight between both hands.

I turn and walk around the chair, putting myself behind Maxwell. He screams for help, knowing that there is no one to hear him. I wish that the last thing I could hear from him was that incredible countertenor, rather than these off-key howls of terror, but the world rarely delivers what you want.

Asher and J. C. are watching me, waiting for some kind of signal that it's okay for them to lace into our Judas. I brace my right knee against the back of the chair and bring the tie over Maxwell's head and around his throat. The silk stretches in my hands as it cuts of Maxwell's air and crushes his trachea.

I nod, and my choir lunges forward like hungry jackals. J. C. plunges his butterfly knife into our betrayer's leg. Asher takes a deep puff of his cigar, getting the tip cherry red before stubbing it out in Maxwell's eye. As for me, I simply pull back on my tie, as hard as I can, thankful that I don't have to look into the face of the boy I'm executing.

No black unicorn appears as I murder my friend. No demon speaks to me. No hidden notes from the music of Hell play in my mind. As Maxwell gurgles, and gasps, and bleeds I know that what's happening right now isn't like what happened with Gravetree, or the family on Raylene Street, or even Leo Wilkins. Maxwell's death is different, and there is no magic or music in it.

CHAPTER 18

A sher and I stare down at the grave we dug for Ashley and Maxwell in a crawlspace beneath the crumbling railway platform. The shared burial plot isn't quite six feet deep, but in the dim light of the crawlspace, barely illuminated by the setting sun, the grave appears fathomless.

It's taken most of the day to excavate the grave. Digging holes, deep holes at least, is tougher work than one might think. We only had a single rusted coal shovel to work with, and our labor was compounded by having to work hunched over in the tight confines of the crawlspace. We needed to do our best to make sure no one stumbles upon the freshly turned earth, and here it will be well hidden.

I crawl out from under the platform and dust myself off. I stretch my aching back and look around the old railway station. The late afternoon sun and the haze of clouds above turns the sky an otherworldly shade of pinkish yellow. Dying leaves rustle in the trees, like flickering ghost flames. A terrible silence hangs over everything. No bugs chirp. No birds sing. There's only the occasional sound of leaves in the wind.

I close my eyes and imagine this is what death must be like. Silence and darkness. A vacuum lacking expression or consciousness. Is that what I've consigned Maxwell to?

I open my eyes and see J. C. lighting a trashcan fire from dried leaves and old wood. It doesn't take long for it to catch. The shifting dimensions of the rising flames hypnotize me. I stare into them and pace around the perimeter of the trashcan, appreciating the fire from every angle. As the orange and yellow tongues lick at the air I am overcome by their grandeur.

The sight stirs something in my soul, and I pray that there is some sort of afterlife, even if it is a place of suffering and flame. One can find beauty in fire and agony, after all. But oblivion? An eternity without music or art? What hell could be worse than that?

Asher now creeps out of the crawlspace. I watch him through the flames of the trash fire. He's shirtless and covered in sweat, despite the chill in the air. His Texas bolo tie hangs about his neck and sticks to the perspiration on his chest. He stands up tall, stretching his back and raising his hands above his head. Streaks of grime, driven down his chest by rivers of sweat, paint dark lines on his flesh. I can't help but note, as he shakes out his dark, mohawked mane, that there is something animalistic about him—something almost equine.

"How are we going to get them from there to here?" J. C. asks, pointing to the boxcar ten yards away.

"We need a tarp or something," Asher

replies. "Something we can wrap them up with and use as a makeshift stretcher."

None of us have thought this far ahead. I scan around for anything we might wrap the corpses in to hide their scent from dogs and avoid painting a trail of blood across the ground.

Nothing catches my eye, however, and it's hard to focus. The sunset colors of the sky paint everything in vivid, unnatural tones. Oppressive silence deafens me. My skin is crawling from the dirt, blood, and grime that covers it. Chills overtake me as the sweat soaking my clothes helps the October air sap the heat from my body.

As I fumble around, dazed and useless, I'm vaguely aware that the others are looking around as well. After a few minutes, Asher yells out that he's found something. His voice sounds muted, as if the dying autumn forest and the dead railway station are trying to silence him. He pops out of a boxcar, a different one from where Maxwell and Ashley lay dead, with a ragged canvas tarp in his arms.

He brings the tarp into the train car where we murdered Maxwell. J. C. and I follow. The three of us unfold the canvas and spread it out across the floor. It's ripped in a dozen places, and soiled with God knows what, but it's what we have.

"We better do them one at a time," J. C. comments, his voice just as distant as Asher's. "Neither one of them ever skipped a meal."

We start with Ashley, or rather the corpse that used to be Ashley. She's closer to the door and closer to the tarp.

Asher grabs both her wrists, while J. C. and I

194

each grab a leg. She's heavy. Even heavier than she looks.

J. C. and Asher had beaten her to death with their fists and feet, so her lacerations are minor, even where one of them carved the word *PIG* into her chest. She doesn't leave much blood behind, but piss drips from her pubic hair, leaving a trail from where she died to the door of the boxcar. Nothing else drips out, and I'm relieved at that. I feared they might have raped her in front of Maxwell before they did her in, and even though he betrayed me, he wouldn't have deserved to go through watching that.

Her body makes a sick thud against the tarp and the wooden floor beneath when we drop her. We wrap her up in the nasty, ancient canvas until she looks like an insect gone into a chrysalis from which she will never emerge. She makes another gross thud, this one a bit wet-sounding, as her bundled-up corpse hits the rusted train door on the ground in front of the car. Once we have her out of the car, Asher takes one side and I take the other. J. C. handles lookout duty as we carry her over to the crawlspace and the makeshift grave beneath.

There's not enough room to carry her beneath the train platform, so we drop her to the ground and drag her the rest of the way. We unwrap the tarp under the platform and roll the ruined waste of Ashley from glee club into the earthen hole.

We return to the boxcar and repeat the process, this time with Maxwell. He's heavier than Ashley by a good margin. Even between the three of us, we barely get him off the ground. His ass scrapes against the dirty wooden floor, and blood trails behind him from numerous wounds that will never heal.

We drop him down on the tarp, and I try not to look his corpse in the face, but I can't help it. One dead eye bulges. The other is burned and ruined. His complexion has turned an ugly purple, and wicked bruises—hangman's bruises—paint his throat a hideous black and blue.

Asher folds one end of the canvas up over Maxwell, and that is the last I ever see of him. We finish wrapping him, then drag him out of the boxcar. It's harder to get him over to the crawlspace. Even wrapped up in the tarp, we can barely keep him high enough off the ground so that he doesn't carve a path in the dirt over to his grave. We manage it, though, and with only a few drops of blood dripping out from the canvas.

When we get back into the crawlspace we don't bother to unwrap him. Instead, we roll him, tarp and all, into the grave and on top of his girlfriend. Bottled-up gas from one or both corpses belches out from one end or another. Asher laughs at the sound.

We take turns with the rusty coal shovel, covering the bodies one scoop of dirt at a time, while the others push mounds of loose soil back into the pit. By the time we finish, it is well past dark. Aside from the trashcan fire J. C. set, there's no light out here. Even the moon is hidden behind dark clouds, unwilling to gaze down at our crime.

With the last bit of dirt tamped down, we huddle around the fire and toss in any clothes that are too obviously stained with blood. I stand shivering in just my jacket and slacks, as both my button-down and undershirt are painted in crimson splatter. They burn in the can, along with the tie that I used to strangle Maxwell and Asher's white blazer and band T-shirt.

Only J. C. is left fully dressed when everything is said and done. His suit has more blood on it than mine, but it doesn't show on his black-on-black ensemble, at least not in the darkness. He'll need to get rid of his suit, of course, just as Asher and I will have to dispose of our remaining clothes. That can wait until we get home, though. The police might find reason to stop to us if we come back into town, strolling the streets filthy and naked. None of us want that.

Asher drops the coal shovel into the fire, letting the flames eat away at the wood and eradicate any DNA.

I take a sip from my flask and hand it to Asher, who after a swallow passes it to J. C. The three of us stand in the narrow warmth and light of the fire and watch it burn to nothing as we drain my gin to the same state.

"Did you hear it?" Asher asks. "While you killed him, did you hear any more of *The Madrigal*?"

I take a drink and stare into the flames without answering.

It's Tuesday night . . . could that be right? Is it still only Tuesday? How the hell does a single day last this long?

It's Tuesday night at who knows what

fucking time. The temperature has dropped near freezing. Goosebumps riddle my filthy skin, still sticky with sweat, and gore, and soil.

J. C. and Asher have both gone home, and I'm currently making my way back to . . . to where I live. That place isn't my home. Raylene Street was my home. The Academy was my home. That sepulcher I dwell in with the ghost of my mother? Not so much.

A squad car creeps past me. The flashers aren't going, and the siren isn't blasting, but it makes me nervous. There's no way they could know about Maxwell or Ashley. They haven't even been gone long enough for their parents to file missing persons reports. Still, I decide to make a detour down the next side street.

I take a right, wondering if the cruiser will follow, if not for what we did today, then for some other crime catching up with me. Maybe they can identify me on the surveillance footage of us stomping Leo Wilkins. Maybe I left some evidence at Raylene Street. God, I don't even know what happened over there. Or perhaps they want to talk about Philip Gravetree.

Fuck.

No. It's nothing.

Fuck!

It's just a patrol car, Lucien. Get a fucking hold of yourself.

Fuck!!!

Get a fucking hold of yourself, maestro.

"Jesus Christ," I mutter to myself. "What the hell did we do?"

What you had to, Amduscias mutters from Hell into my heart.

My breath comes in short gasps. I keep looking back over my shoulder, sure that the police are ready to roll up on me at any moment. Maybe they should. Maybe that would be for the best.

Master Beaumont, please don't think such a thought. We both know that true art is with great pain wrought.

I turn right again at the next corner, desperate to put some further distance between that cruiser and myself, even as I consider turning myself in.

"I don't want to do this anymore," I mutter aloud. "I don't want to hurt anyone else. I don't want to go to prison. You can keep the damn song."

I say the words, but I don't know that I mean them. *The Madrigal* plays in my head, haunting and alluring in its fragmentary beauty. To hear it in its entirety, even once—would that not be worth jail, or death, or even the end of the world?

I shake the thought from my head, hoping to silence the music as well, but I can't. It plays louder. It plays at concert-level decibels, breaking apart any decency within me that won't yield to it. Reason, will, empathy—they all shatter like crystal before the high note singing in my mind.

I look up and that's when I see it at the end of the street— a church, erected in the Romanesque style, its stone façade a beacon of strength. Stray beams of light penetrate through the bright stained glass, promising warmth and sanctuary. The demon can't follow me there, can he?

The soles of my shoes slap against the

cobblestone sidewalk, echoing like gunshots in the empty street. My pace has no meter to it, and I stumble as I rush forward. The weight of the day saps my strength, and I find myself wondering if I'll even make it to the church. Every muscle aches. Throbbing pain radiates from the back of my skull all the way to my eyeballs. My lungs burn, and my legs are jelly.

That place holds nothing for you, Master Beaumont. It's a house of rot and dread.

I want to tell the demon to fuck off, but I'm already gasping for breath as I run. If Amduscias can read my mind, which I'm sure it can, then it gets the message.

It's only when I reach the stone steps of the church that I slow my pace. My thighs tremble and burn as I walk up the staircase. The seven steps feel like seven hundred.

When I reach the top of the stairs, I shamble to the oaken double doors and take a moment to appreciate the intricacy of the brass hinges and decorative bracings that adorn them. I tug at the massive handles, expecting the doors to open wide and some holy light to bathe and cleanse me. The doors don't budge, though.

The good Lord can't answer the door, Master Beaumont. The good Lord, he is dead.

I fall to my knees before God's threshold, filthy, exhausted, and reeking of the foulest sins. Tears drip from my eyes, leaving streaks down my grime-caked face. My heart and head pound in unison.

There are no more fathers to guide you.

There is no reason to be had.

I pound my fist against the door, more out of frustration than of hope that someone might open up. I've been left out in the cold—left alone—enough times to know when no one is going to answer.

In a world where order has crumbled, to be sane is to be mad.

The pain in my skull intensifies. I press my palms against my eyeballs, afraid that the pulsing ache in my head will pop them out if I don't hold them in. Maybe I should let it happen. Let my eyes shoot out from my skull in the hope that Amduscias pours out behind them, the way ancient doctors would drill holes in their patients' skulls to relieve them of demons.

There's nothing left to do but sing as you descend.

I fall onto my side. The cold stone kisses my cheek. Rainbow light from the stained-glass windows teases my skin but offers no warmth. I realize that this isn't God's house. It's his tomb. Amduscias is right. God is dead, and he can't forgive me.

And there's no song left to sing but The Madrigal of the World's End.

No one can.

CHAPTER 19

It's noon by the time I wake up. For a moment my mind grants me the small mercy of believing that yesterday was a nightmare, that I had merely dreamt of murdering Maxwell and burying him in a shared grave atop his girlfriend. It's a fleeting mercy that vanishes as the reality of what we've done comes flooding back.

I sit up in bed, unsure how I even got there. Getting home is a blur, and I must have come in and passed out. I'm still in the same clothes. Still grimy with earth, blood, and sweat. Dirt penetrates deep down under my fingernails, deeper than it seems it should be able to go. My hair is a matted rat's nest.

First things being first, I pick out some music to clean up to. Something calming, to set my nerves to rest. Dvořák seems the man for the job, and I start things off with his *Czech Suite.*

With music in place, I head to the bathroom, where I strip down to nothing and turn the shower knob as far to the right as it will go. As the water heats up, I trim down my fingernails, clipping them so short that it's painful. The filth-encrusted nail clippings fall into the open toilet, where I flush them away.

I throw back the curtain and step into the searing shower. The heat feels good. The pain feels good. It makes me feel clean.

Streams of black and brown run down my body. I soap up a face cloth and scrub at my skin. I scour until it hurts, then I keep going harder. I scrub my ears and inside my nostrils. I let the smells of soil, sweat, and death dissolve beneath the shower's spray. The generic clean scent of Dollar Store bar soap and the counterfeit coconut fragrance of our cheap shampoo perfumes my sins and transgressions.

I stand there under the spray, long after the water circling the drain has gone from murky brown to clear. I let the water go cold, not wanting to face the world on the other side of the shower curtain. When I finally do step out, I find that the mirror, still shattered from when I lashed out at it, is painted in condensation. I don't bother wiping it away. There's nothing beneath there worth seeing.

Not much thought goes into laying out my clothes when I get back to my room. Charcoal suit. White shirt. Plain black tie—the first things I pull down from the closet. I put them on, and all I can think is that Maxwell deserved to be buried in something better than he was.

My appetite is non-existent, but after I'm dressed I toast a few slices of bread and brew a cup of French Vanilla tea. I nibble at my food and absent-mindedly thumb through the mail on the table, wondering what my life is now.

An offer for car insurance.

Am I going to prison? Is it all over?

Electrical shut-off notice.

Should I just get the hell out of Enfield? Just run for my life and pick up the pieces wherever I land?

A seasonal program schedule from the Boston Symphony Orchestra.

What would Father do?

He'd do the gallows dance, says an evil voice in my head. I can't tell if they are the demon's words or my own.

I toss the mail aside and get up from the table.

I pick up my phone and dial the Academy. I haven't talked to Mr. Larson in months, since the end of last school year, and even as the phone rings I don't know what I'll say. A receptionist picks up after three rings. I ask her to connect me to the headmaster. The person on the other end asks who's calling, then puts me on hold. A minute passes, and the same voice returns to the line, telling me that Mr. Larson isn't taking any calls right now. I hang up and throw my phone across the room.

He's just another whore, like Ms. Kane. Another role model for hire, only interested in you for as long as they're paid to be. All prostitute pleasantries with no genuine affection or consideration.

I burst into tears and get up from the table.

I stride to Mother's eternally closed bedroom door and rest my head against it. A memory comes to me from before Father died—from before everything was such a mess. I'm in the yard, burning ants with a magnifying glass, watching them smoke and cook. Mother catches me, but she doesn't yell or scream. She doesn't slap me or take away my toy. She explains those ants have families, and that they take care of one another and bury their dead. She tells me they have feelings and experience pain and asks how I would feel if some giant came and set my family on fire. That was the last time I ever hurt an ant.

Mother's broken now, of course. She has been since long before Father's death. But prior to the drugs and the cheating and all the horrible shit we've been through, my mother held some modicum of wisdom, and I could sure as hell use it right now.

"Mom?" I ask, knocking on her bedroom door.

There's no answer. I knock again, louder this time.

"Mom, I'm in trouble, and I don't know what to do."

For another minute there's only silence, but then I hear sheets stirring and clumsy stumbling. I hear her coming to the door.

"I need someone to tell me it's wrong to burn ants," I whisper.

The doorknob jiggles, and my heart skips a beat. For the first time in years I want to crawl into my mother's arms and beg her to make things right. I want her to stroke my hair and promise to keep the demons at bay. When the door opens it's not my mother on the other side, though.

"Your mother's asleep, kid," says the naked stranger standing in the doorway to her bedroom. He's old and flabby and covered in blurry tattoos. Putrid breath and stray spit passes between his missing teeth as he talks.

He closes the door in my face.

Fuck Mother and her drunken, whoring, nihilism. Fuck Violet Sarkissian, with her wasted talent and ingratitude. Fuck Amduscias, that manipulative nightmare, who led my father and me to the gates of Hell.

Today I leave them all behind. Today is my last day in Enfield. These are the things I tell myself, unaware of how untrue they are. I'll never actually leave this town again, but I don't know that yet.

My big military-style backpack, the one I used to take the essentials to the Academy when I went there and to bring them back when I left, is filled once again with just the necessities. Three dress shirts—white, blue, and black. Three ties. Three pairs of slacks. Five sets of underwear and socks. A toothbrush. A notebook, songbook, and pens. Business cards for Father's industry contacts. And a Leatherman for defense and utility.

I've scraped together all the cash I could find around the house, then drained what little I could from Mother's account. Altogether I have about three hundred dollars, which is enough to get me to New York, where I can try to find some work among Father's contacts, even if it's just as an usher or something. I don't care what it is, as long as I get the hell out of Enfield.

Currently I'm walking against the tide of students rushing out of Swift River High after the final bell of the day. My bobblehead Beethoven, the one that Maxwell bought me, is in my locker, and it's important that I take it with me. I loved Maxwell, and I miss him, and even though we put him in the ground for his betrayal, I think a part of him—or at least a symbol of what we had—deserves to leave this place.

The crowd thins the deeper I get into the school. As I walk down the hall to my locker, I see only see a few stragglers. An ugly couple is making out beneath a stairwell. Rowdy cheerleaders pass by on their way to practice, showing off their toned, flexible bodies in compensation for their weak and rigid minds. An underclassman I don't recognize, dressed in a black pinstripe suit, walks by and nods at me with a smirk.

I turn and watch the younger boy walk away, wondering why he's dressed like that and if I should know him. Only my choir dresses with any semblance of class or style, and he is not one of us.

"I don't get it either, little mini-nerds copping your style, but I guess it's a thing."

I turn around and see Ari Cole exiting the boy's room with two of his troglodyte football buddies.

"Of all the people they could imitate, they choose you and your jerk off friends?"

My locker is only fifteen feet away. All I have to do is grab my little plastic Beethoven and leave, then I will never have to see Ari fucking Cole again. I will never have to hear his slurred, idiot voice or look into his dead eyes. All I have to do is ignore him one last time.

But I don't. I flip him off with both hands.

"Enjoy your empty little life in this empty little town."

I turn and walk toward my locker, but I don't make it far. One of them punches me in the back of the skull. I drop to the ground, dizzy and hurt. Ari kicks me in the ribs. His friends laugh as he crouches down next to me and screams in my face.

"You think you're better than me with your nerdy-ass suits and faggot silk ties? Think you're better than me 'cause you can sing and 'cause you skipped a grade? You think you're better than me because you used to have money till your old man offed himself?"

He brings his open hand high into the air and smacks me in the face so hard that my head bounces off the linoleum floor. The world is a spinning blur, but I can make out people watching. Some of them look uncomfortable. Some are laughing. A few are taking video on their phones.

"Let's see who's better than who," Ari laughs before telling his friends to take me into the bathroom.

They drag me by my feet. I yell for help. The couple under the stairs look down at their feet. The cheerleaders laugh and point. The young kid in the suit runs away. A handwritten sign decrying that *There's No Place Like Homecoming* is the last thing I see before the bathroom door closes, leaving me alone with Ari and his thugs.

I struggle for escape, clawing at the floor. My fingers find purchase on the rough grout between the tiles, but it's no use. Ari and his friends just drag me back.

Pain envelops my being as I'm met with a hail of punches and kicks. My chin slams into the hard tile and splits open. The toe of a sneaker swells my eye shut. Bones crunch in my hand as a heel comes down on it. Everything becomes surreal as agony overloads my senses.

Bile floods my mouth as I retch from a kick to the stomach. I belch out a stream of puke, which gets on Ari's sneakers. This pisses him off more, and he kicks me even harder, yelling that I owe him a new pair of shoes.

The beating slows, then finally stops, and they carry me into a stall. They pull the straps of my backpack down over my arms and force my head into the toilet. My face hits the cold water, and I thrash with panic as they submerge my head. I try to stand up, but someone kicks my legs out from under me. Muffled laughter comes from just above the water.

Unable to hold my breath any longer, I take in a lungful of toilet water, just before someone pulls me up by my hair. I choke and gag and gasp. They yell taunts and make jokes that I'm not cognizant enough to make out, then shove my face back into the cold, septic water. This happens twice more, and each time I'm sure I'll drown.

Ari and his thugs let go of me. I pull my head from the toilet and gasp for air. Behind me, something is happening. There is banging, screaming, and swearing. It's a chaotic mess, and I can't make sense of it until I turn and see Asher, J. C., and that young kid in the pinstripes brawling with Ari's crew.

One of Ari's idiot friends is on the ground,

holding his thigh and screaming. Asher is standing above him with a bloody pocket knife. The other football player misses with a haymaker at the kid in pinstripes and smashes his fist into the tile wall. J. C. isn't faring as well as the others, though. Ari is repeatedly smashing his head into a metal stall. His forehead splits open, and blood cascades down his face.

I shrug off my backpack and fumble for my Leatherman. Within a few seconds I have it in my hand. It pays to be organized.

I flip open the serrated blade of the multitool and stumble toward Ari, ready to bury it in his neck. That's when Mr. Brodsky and Mr. Jackson bust in.

"What in the hell is going on here?"

Everyone stops as if we'd been caught in Medusa's gaze. I drop my blade, and Asher does the same. All is silent, save for the strangely syncopated rhythm of our heavy, collective breathing.

We're all crammed into the principal's office—my choir, the kid in the pinstripe suit, and Ari with his goons. I tell Brodsky how they dragged me into the bathroom and kicked my ass. I tell him that the cheerleaders have video of it happening. Pinstripe suit kid, who is named Peter Downing, backs up my story and tells Brodsky that he grabbed J. C. and Asher to come help me.

The football players have a different story. Ari tells the principal that we jumped him and his two friends in the bathroom while they were minding their own business. Brodsky takes them at their word and dismisses them without so much as a detention. Ari gives me a smirk as he leaves the office, and the opening notes of *The Madrigal* thunder in my ears.

Mr. Brodsky reams us all out, then tells us we're expelled for violence and gang activity. Asher yells back at him and calls him on his bullshit. J. C. tries to reason with him. The underclassman who's trying to dress like us, this poor kid whom we don't even know, is on the verge of hyperventilating.

I just sit back and listen to the music in my head. It's no longer a collection of *oohs* and *ahhs* creating melody and counterpoint. I can hear more and more of the lyrics—the poetry of the world's end—in my mind. It is not in English but in some ancient language, older than Latin or Aramaic and far more graceful. Still, I understand its meaning and even the subtext of expression.

I also hear the percussion behind the melody. Rapid-fire double bass. The powerful, cracking downbeat of the snare drum. A steady and constant rhythm on the ride cymbal. It's the rhythm of death and war.

Mr. Brodsky tells us the cops are coming to arrest us on weapons charges and insinuates that they'll probably want to talk to us about a lot more.

"You don't know the half of it," I tell him.

J. C. and Asher stare at me in disbelief. I stand up and motion for them to follow. Brodsky commands us to sit back down. He tells us we can't leave until the police are here.

"They know how to find us," I say, leaving the office. Asher gets up first and follows me out.

J. C. does the same, though he straggles a few steps behind. The kid in pinstripes stays put, which is fine. He might dress the part, but he's not one of us.

Brodsky chases us down the hall, shouting. We ignore him and make our way out of the school, not running away but walking with grace and confidence—shoulders back and heads held high. At least I am, anyway. I can't see how the others are composing themselves behind me.

"Brodsky's got us fucking made, Lucien." Asher shout-whispers. "What are we gonna do?"

We pass another sign for the homecoming dance, decorated with construction paper turkeys. It's tonight. I would have been in New York by then if they had just let me be. But they didn't, and they'll all be there. Violet fucking Sarkissian will be performing with the glee club. Ari Cole and his goons will be chasing cheerleaders. And, of course, there'll be faculty. Maybe Mr. Brodsky, who gave the football players a free pass after kicking the shit out of me. Maybe Mr. Jackson, who punished me for having my clothes pissed on. Maybe Ms. Kane, who dropped me like a bad habit.

"The only thing left for us, Asher. I finish *The Madrigal,* and then we perform it."

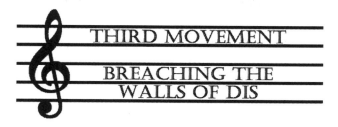

CHAPTER 20

There's a card from the local police—a Detective Carl Cho—taped to my front door when I get home. The words *call me* are written across the blank space at the top in blue pen. Fat Chance.

I unlock the door and step in. The kitchen reeks of vinegar. A charred, bent spoon sits next to a used syringe on the counter. It would seem Mother's bedroom guest had something to offer beyond his charm and good looks.

I drop my backpack on the table and retrieve the songbook for *The Madrigal of the World's End,* along with a pen. It's heavier than a notebook should be, but it does carry the key to Hell within it. I suppose there is a weight to a thing such as that.

"I'm ready to finish this," I say, drawing the head of a black unicorn upon the songbook, just as Gravetree's copy had on its cover. I render the demon alive with each crude line of detail. I invoke and summon it, like a suburban Solomon.

"Let me hear it all."

The penned bust of Amduscias turns out of profile and glares at me. Its beard and mane billow and inky smoke puffs from its nostrils.

"Are you finally ready, Master Beaumont? To sing the song no sane man would dare?"

"Great art is not born without sacrifice," I answer.

"Deliver what your father wouldn't, and I will sing every note in your ear."

The demon's voice is music and agony. It's the suffering of Beethoven, staring at compositions he would only ever hear in his mind. It's a condemned man's final cigarette as he considers the firing squad before him.

I tuck the songbook into the back of my pants, put the pen in my pocket, and grab the syringe off the table before heading into to the bathroom. I don't bother turning on the light as I enter. The illumination from the next room is enough for me to navigate by, and the last thing I want is to catch a glimpse of my reflection. I know what kind of shape I'm in without needing it confirmed by the broken mirror. One eye is purple and swollen. An ugly little flap of skin hangs from my chin. My broken left hand is wrapped up with my tie, like a silk ace bandage. The suit I'm wearing does little to cancel out the indignity of my mangled state.

In the cabinet below the sink is a bottle of concentrated bleach. I crouch down, an effort that rewards me with agony in all the places I'd been stomped on, and retrieve the bottle. Standing back up is just as painful. I stab the bottle with the sharp and pull back the plunger. Bleach fills the vacuum of the syringe—a hundred units of chlorine. I toss the bottle into the tub and stroll out of the bathroom.

On the way through the living room, I glance at the Monet prints on the wall. Mother never even noticed how I ruined them. I walk past my little out of tune piano with the army of empty gin bottles lined on top of it and over to Mother's door. It's closed, just as it always is. Just like her heart. I won't miss any of it.

The door is unlocked. I turn the knob and push it inward. The space beyond is a rathole of filth and clutter. Fruit flies swarm around the towers of crusty dishes and stacked glasses on Mother's nightstand. A carpet of soiled clothes and used tissues hides the floor beneath. Empty amber pill bottles litter the floor. Some have her name on the label, but many don't.

She lies in her bed, naked and face down in her pillow. Her breath is shallow and uneven. There's a yellow tinge to her complexion, and her flesh seems as if it's sagging off her skeleton. It's been some time since I've actually looked at her, and I didn't realize quite how badly she was doing.

Her wretched drug hookup and fuckbuddy is gone. It's a shame. It would have been no small pleasure to kill him as well.

I walk around the bed, stumbling through the piles of dirty laundry, and sit down next to her. I take her hand in mine, following the track marks with my eyes.

"You were so mad at him for stepping into that noose, but you didn't save him, the way he saved you. You were so pissed at him for dying, but you followed him into death. You burned everything good in you on his funeral pyre."

I find a vein and inject the syringe into her arm with my good hand.

"I suppose all three of us died that night. Father was just the only one with the good sense to quit walking around."

Chlorine floods my mother's bloodstream as I depress the plunger. There's no going back. I move from the bed and pull the songbook for *The Madrigal* out from the back of my pants. I plop my ass down in a pile of dirty clothes, click my pen, and wait for the music to flood my mind.

In less than a minute Mother is seizing. Four choked gasps issue from her in succinct rhythm, counting off the choir of Hell to sing *The Madrigal* for me. I watch her die as the music plays, jotting down the missing parts as they come. A stray note of discord here. An unexpected triplet there. It's moving and enchanting.

It takes a while for Mother to die, and it's quite a painful-looking spectacle, even though she is unconscious. She gurgles and twitches for the better part of *The Madrigal,* only stopping in the middle of the final movement. When she does expire, though— when death takes hold and her soul descends to Hell—the music stops.

I look down at my songbook. Vacuous missing notes and measures from the final movement stare back up at me. The song remains incomplete.

"You said the song would be mine if I killed her." My voice is an angry whisper.

"Are you finally ready, Master Beaumont? To sing the song no sane man would dare? Deliver what your father wouldn't, and I will sing every note

in your ear."

"That's what I did!" I scream at the air, rising to my feet.

"Deliver what your father wouldn't," the demon repeats again.

"Me? You want me?" My voice is trembling with anger and frustration.

"Great art is not born without sacrifice."

I nod to the Demon's invisible presence. It's clear to me now, looking upon my mother's body, remembering Maxwell's last breaths, and knowing what Amduscias ultimately demands of me, that *The Madrigal* was never mine. I never possessed it. *The Madrigal* possesses me . . . and I'm okay with that.

I turn my back on Mother, dead in her horrid little bedroom. It's time to prepare for the first and final performance of *The Madrigal of the World's End*—an iconic piece of culture, destined to put Enfield on the map. One show, standing room only.

My clothes are a mess of blood, sweat, and toilet water. I cast them off and don my finest suit. Black, virgin silk. Single-breasted jacket with two buttons and double-vented in the back. Four-button matching vest. Classic trousers with French pockets in the front and button welt in the back. I pair the suit with a tailored silk shirt, complete with French cuffs.

I choose a burgundy pocket square with white stripes and a matching tie. I find that matching your tie and pocket square is a bit much for most occasions, but tonight demands formality. My gunmetal tie clip and Father's obsidian cufflinks complete the ensemble.

It's a struggle to put on my tie with one hand

broken. After three failed attempts I just let it hang across my neck like a scarf. I know that most people wouldn't put any care into how they looked as their lives crumbled around them, but I intend to meet the end of the world on my own terms. Or as close as I can, anyway.

Disappointed about the tie and loath to look at my tattered flesh in the mirror, I'm otherwise pleased with my final state of dress. There is nary a man who might leave a better-dressed corpse.

To avoid the cops tracking me through GPS, I dumped my phone on the way home. I told Asher and J. C. to do the same, which means we have no means of contact. I can only hope that they retrieved the instruments for our performance. I suppose I'll know soon enough. We're to meet in two hours to recruit Maxwell's replacement for the choir.

CHAPTER 21

There's only one singer I know of in Enfield with the range and talent to take Maxwell's place, and we are parked outside her house. It's a miracle of Hell that the cops didn't pick up J. C. and Asher on their way here. I'm sure they were not inconspicuous, walking across town in black suits with a massive duffle bag. I, at least, had the camouflage of Mother's stolen car. All they had was a bit of luck and the blessing of Amduscias.

Asher rifles through the duffle bag in the back seat. He hands a pistol to J. C. and another to me. The weapons are different from one another but roughly the same size. I don't know about guns, so fuck if I can say what caliber or make it is. It's heavier than it looks, but it does carry the power of death within it. I suppose there is a weight to a thing such as that.

"Where's yours, Asher?" I ask.

"I'm saving the big one for later, and my brother only had the two pistols in his gun safe," he says.

Cold power flows from the gun's grip, flooding my soul. It feels the way *The Madrigal* sounds. That makes sense, I suppose. An instrument becomes an extension of the song it plays.

"You sure this is the move, Lucien?" Asher questions.

"Do you know anyone else who can sing Maxwell's part?"

"I guess not."

Asher reaches back into the duffle bag and hands out packs of disposable earplugs. I look at them with confusion.

"We don't want to fuck up our hearing before we sing tonight."

I nod and squeeze down the little foam plugs. They expand as I place them in my ears, filtering the sound around me rather than blocking it.

J. C. pulls back the slide on his pistol. It makes a satisfying click, and we all get out of the car.

"Wait a minute, Lucien," J. C. says. "You can't pick up your date looking like that, maestro."

He tucks his pistol into his waistband, leans in close to me, and pops up the collar of my shirt. My tie hangs over my neck like a scarf. J. C. takes it and ties a double Windsor for me, something I was unable to do with my broken hand.

"Thank you," I say, sincerely touched by the sentiment.

"Hey, we gotta look our best tonight, right?" he says with a wink.

A brick pathway leads from the sidewalk to the front door of the Sarkissian house. Dying purple flowers, victims of the autumn cold, line either side of the walkway, protruding up through mounds of brittle leaves. Two columns rise up on either side of the entrance, framing the door like some ancient gate.

We saunter down the path, the soles of our shoes clicking against the brick in a musical rhythm. When we get to the door Asher ducks to the left of it and pulls a switchblade from his pocket. I hide over to the right. J. C. takes center stage in front of the door, since he's currently the most presentable. Violet's parents might not open the door if they saw my battered face or Asher's mohawk and lunatic grin. J. C.'s hair covers up the gash on his forehead from our fight at school, and he looks mostly respectable. Maybe a bit Addams Family, in his black three-piece suit with matching shirt and tie, but respectable nonetheless.

He knocks three times, then puts his hands behind his back to hide his instrument. The door opens. From inside I hear a masculine voice saying *hello* but like a question rather than a salutation. J. C. swings the gun from behind his back and fires two shots.

J. C. steps into the house, then Asher and I come out of our hiding spots to follow behind. A severe-looking man with salt-and-pepper hair and leathery, olive skin lies dead on the other side of the threshold. Blood pumps out of his chest, saturating his Patriots jersey and pooling on the living-room floor. His lifeless eyes stare up at the ceiling, a look of shock engraved upon his face.

We all sidestep the body and manage to avoid walking through the blood as we enter. A panicked voice—Violet's voice—is calling from upstairs, asking if everything is okay. I motion toward the staircase, and we move as one. Before we reach the stairs someone else—someone young and feminine from the sound of it—calls from beyond the doorway of the living room.

"Bob? What was that?"

A woman steps into the living room. She's fit and gorgeous, in a very manufactured way. Her hair and nails are immaculate despite the casual outfit of a crop top and yoga pants she wears. My guess is that she's not a day over twenty-five. Something tells me she isn't Violet's real mother.

"Nice piece of ass, Mr. Sarkissian," J. C. says, giving a thumbs-up to the man exsanguinating on the floor.

She screams, a harsh and ugly cry. I raise my pistol and aim it at her chest. Her scream becomes a muffled sob. She's too panicked to beg for her life, so her eyes do the pleading. She doesn't want to die. She'd probably do anything to avoid it. Give up her body. Give up Violet's body. I'm not here for a body, though. I'm here for a voice.

I pull the trigger, not knowing what kind of recoil to expect. The kickback is less than I would have thought, and in less time than it takes for that reflection, Mr. Sarkissian's trophy wife is dead on the ground. It's all a bit anticlimactic, but that's okay. The curtain hasn't even risen for the night. There's still plenty of time for proper drama.

"Come on, before she calls the cops!" Asher yells. The two of them are already rushing up the stairs as I gaze at the pistol in my hand, pondering the ease and lack of dramatic tension in the murder I've just committed. He's right, of course; this is no time to wax philosophical. I turn and follow my choir up the stairs.

CURTIS M. LAWSON

J. C. is wrestling with a doorknob to the only closed door in the second-floor hallway. Asher nudges him aside and kicks the door hard. The frame splits a bit, but it doesn't give. He raises his knee up to his chest and kicks again, this time with everything he's got. The door bursts open, and a shrill scream issues from within the room.

"They're in my bedroom!" she screams. "Help!"

Asher steps through the broken doorway, carving the air with his switchblade. J. C. follows with his gun held out above Asher's shoulder. I can't see in the room from where I am, but I hear crying as Asher demands the phone.

A few seconds later I'm in Violet Sarkissian's bedroom, and I find myself lightheaded. The room smells like her, and it looks like her. That's not quite right, I suppose. It doesn't look like her but rather an expression of her. A canopy bed draped with magenta lace curtains sits in the center of the room—a heart of sensual elegance and class. Surrounding this centerpiece, this core of Violet's bedroom, are tacky posters of pop stars, gaudy, plastic trophies, and stacks of garbage books and records.

This place, Violet's little slice of the world, is like a symbol of her very being, so beautiful and powerful at the core but encumbered with the wretched trappings pushed on her by a world that fears greatness. How she could shine if she shed the bindings of our modern anti-culture. I suppose I'm here to help her do just that.

Asher knocks the phone from Violet's hand

and crushes it beneath his booted heel. She swings at him, but he catches her by the wrist. He squeezes hard enough to elicit a yelp of pain, then presses the flat of his blade against her cheek.

"Lucien wants you alive," he says. "Don't make me disappoint him."

"Good evening, Violet," I say, meaning it as best I can under the circumstances.

Her clenched eyelids unleash a torrent of tears. It smears her mascara, leaving winding trails of black down her cheeks. Her lips push out in a childish pout that trembles as she weeps. Her posture falters as if her spine has turned to gelatin.

Even as terrified as Violet is, perhaps more so because of it, she is an absolute vision. She was prepared for the dance before we arrived, dying boyfriend be damned. Her raven hair falls about her shoulders in bouncy curls, and her nails are freshly lacquered the color of her namesake. A little black dress with a mesh neckline, dotted with ebony hearts, hugs her body enough to be alluring, without being lewd. Her makeup is smeared, but I wouldn't say ruined. There's something almost sexy about the wavy black lines going down her cheeks.

"We aren't here to hurt you."

I reach out and stroke her face. A fat, mascara-stained teardrop sticks to my finger. I bring it to my mouth, savoring the salty taste.

"We need you to sing with us tonight. You can do that, can't you?"

Her crying intensifies. Tremors ripple through her entire body, and she nearly collapses. Asher gives her wrist a twist, forcing her to stay on her feet.

"We haven't much time to rehearse, I'm afraid, but you can use my score. I shouldn't need it. I know the song by heart now."

I motion with my pistol that it's time to go. Asher wrenches Violet's arm behind her back, presses his switchblade against her side, and tells her to walk. She does as she's told.

It almost makes me sad, the lack of fight in her. Part of me wants to see her thrash, and claw, and curse at us. I want to see fire and fury in her eyes. But she just cries and walks where Asher leads.

When we get down the stairs, when Violet sees the corpses of her father and her stepmom, or whoever that woman I killed was, she wails, then sobs, then pukes. Asher is yelling at her, telling her that we don't have time for this. J. C. threatens to put a bullet in her head if she doesn't move. She doesn't respond but keeps crying and retching.

I know how it feels to find your father's corpse. I know what a terrible shock it can be, and I know that it will take more than threats to snap her out of this fit.

I fire a shot into Mr. Sarkissian's corpse, right in the chest where they can cover it up beneath a suit for his funeral. The new wound produces almost no blood, as most of it has already spilled across the floor. The sound of the gunfire silences everyone. Asher and J. C. stop shouting threats. Violet stops crying and puking. They all just stare at me.

"You want him to have an open casket, Violet? Get your act together and march out to the car, or the next round goes in his face."

She closes her eyes, chokes back a belch that sounds as if it's full of sick, and starts walking toward the door. Her eyes are lifted to the ceiling as she moves forward. She doesn't want to look at her father. I get it, I suppose. It's a grim thing to bear witness to. At the same time, I sense that she's robbing herself of something special. This is the last time she'll ever see him. Even if she makes it through tonight, through the homecoming dance and *The Madrigal of the World's End,* this is her last chance for a proper look at the man. The piece of meat at his wake will look like a poor wax-museum replica of the real thing.

I stop before we get to the door and tell Violet she can say goodbye if she wishes. That she can kiss his cheek and hold his hand one last time. She shudders and keeps walking. So be it. It's her choice.

Asher leads Violet around her father's corpse. The pool of blood around him is too wide to avoid now, and Violet grimaces at the splashing noise her heels make as she steps through the gore.

We cross the threshold of her shattered home and step into the cold homecoming night. I flip the lock on the knob and close the door behind us. I'd ask Violet if she has her keys, but it doesn't matter. None of us are ever going home.

CHAPTER 22

The homecoming dance is well underway by the time we pull into the parking lot of Swift River High. A giant banner decries *Homecoming* in letters of purple and gold—the school colors. Cars pack the parking lot, mostly empty, but a few with teenage couples doing what teenage couples do in dark cars. If they stay out here long enough they'll miss our performance, which will give the term *getting lucky* a whole new meaning.

No doubt Violet's glee club friends are inside, panicking about her absence. No doubt Mrs. Resnick is wringing her hands, wondering where her star is. Donny Hammond, that ridiculous fashion queer, is pissing his skinny jeans, afraid that Violet won't make it in time to perform whatever garbage pop cover they have planned. They aren't worthy of the music she'll perform with us tonight, nor will they appreciate it.

Violet is in the back seat, pleading with her wrists bound together with plastic zipties. She's telling me that we don't have to do whatever I have planned. She begs us to let her go and promises not to tell the cops it was us who killed her parents. I tell her that lies are ugly and that I only want beauty to come from her mouth tonight. I tell her to shut up and study the score, which she holds awkwardly in her bound hands.

I drive the car around to the back of the school, sticking tight to the wall, to where the double doors leading out of the gym let out. There are three kids smoking cigarettes or maybe joints back there. They're leaning against the doors where I need to park, so no one can run out through the back of the gym.

I flash my high beams at them and beep. Bathed in the light of my headlamps, I recognize one of them as a friend of Ari Cole—one of the kids who dragged me into the bathroom this afternoon. He gives me the finger and keeps smoking.

I rev the engine, then gun it. The tires screech and smoke as we lurch forward. The side mirror scrapes against the brick the wall of the school and snaps off as I race toward the three of them. Two manage to run off to the side. Ari's friend, the piece-of-shit football player who took so much joy in beating my ass, freezes like a deer on the highway. The bumper hits him at knee level, and he flies up onto the hood, shattering the windshield.

Violet screeches. I tell her to save her voice. Asher and J. C. laugh at this, but I didn't mean it to be funny.

I whip the car around, throwing the football player from the hood, then back up slowly into the double doors, not stopping until I hear the bumper crack. Confident that no one will be escaping through there, I kill the engine, snap the key off in the ignition, and pull up the emergency brake.

"Those other kids got away," J. C. says.

"They can run . . ." I say, confident that I needn't finish the idiom.

We all get out of the car, though Violet needs some help from Asher, what with her hands bound and all. I toss the FOB as far as I can into the darkness surrounding the school, then walk over to the huddled form of the boy I just ran down.

He's still alive, moaning and trying to crawl away. I bring my foot down on his ankle. There's a snapping noise, and his foot splays out ninety degrees. Asher comes up behind me and hands me his switchblade.

"I'll unpack the hardware if you wanna deal with him," he offers.

"Gladly."

I take a moment to get a feel for the knife, as Asher warns Violet to stay where she is. I let my hand get used to the grip. It doesn't feel as good as the gun, but it will be quieter, and it isn't quite showtime yet. I straddle the boy's back, pull his head up by a fistful of dirty blond hair, and drag the knife from one ear to the other. Blood shoots out with the force of a fire hose, and he stops moving within seconds.

I flick the gore from the blade and turn to my choir. Always in such good humor, J. C. is smiling and full of nervous energy. Asher is stoic and severe as he unpacks his father's assault rifle from the duffle bag in the trunk. Even Violet, as reluctant as she is to sing with us, exudes a bygone beauty and class that is anathema to this uninspired place and time. It will be an honor to end the world with them.

If only Maxwell could be here with us.

Asher pulls out a gas can from Mother's trunk. It makes a swishing sound as he shakes it. He raises his eyebrow, and you can almost see the light bulb above his head.

"Fuck yeah!" J. C. says, then starts rustling through the backseat for the empty wine bottle we left there on the night we fucked up Leo Wilkins. Seconds later he emerges with it.

Asher fills the bottle with gasoline. I pluck the clip-on tie from the dead football player and hand it to him. He soaks it in gasoline, then stuffs it into the neck of the bottle and passes it to J. C.

"Lucien, we can't do this," Violet says, fighting to keep her voice calm.

"It's a bit late to back out," I say.

"Look! The final movement isn't finished. There are notes missing. Entire phrases are just blank." Her tone is filled with condescension. It's the tone of a person trying to reason with a lunatic. I find it insulting, but there's no time to make a thing of it. The curtain goes up in a few minutes.

"The end is a surprise, even to me," I assure her. "Amduscias will transcribe the music straight upon our souls when the time comes to sing it."

"Who's Amduscias?" she asks, still fighting to keep her cool.

I don't answer. Instead, I look out into the woods behind the school. *In the darkness, amongst the leafless trees, the black unicorn watches, along with my father and Philip Gravetree. This night belongs to us all.*

J. C. and I reload our pistols, and Asher locks a banana clip into his assault rifle. I clear my throat and sing a few notes until I find middle C. Asher and J. C. match my note. Violet does as well, but only after I nudge her in the belly with my gun. We sound good together. We sound damn good.

Asher is to my left, M16 slung over his shoulder. J. C. is to my right, armed with a pistol and a Molotov cocktail. We loop back around to the front of the building, marching in lockstep, with Violet walking in front of us. I have my gun pressed against her spine as a gentle reminder not to run off or play heroine.

There are no students by the front doors, only a lone teacher. Mr. Jackson of all people. It's his job to take tickets and make sure no one wanders in who shouldn't. He's about as observant as he is skilled as a teacher, looking down at his phone, biting into a licorice whip.

I call out his name, wanting him to see who brings his death. He glances up, and anger washes over his face as he recognizes us. I imagine he thought he'd seen the last of me.

I wrap my right arm around Violet's waist, pulling her close to me, and swing my pistol around her body. She flinches and yelps as I fire a single shot at Mr. Jackson. He falls backward, dropping his phone and his licorice.

Violet is weeping again as we approach the teacher's prone body. There's a hole in his chest—a ragged O weeping blood.

"Now *that* is a scarlet letter, Mr. Jackson."

We step around the dead English teacher, beneath the welcoming homecoming banner, and into the halls of Swift River High School. I can hear the music and the spectacle of the dance, even this far from the gym. The noise travels through the halls, beckoning us—challenging us to silence it and perform our own song.

We stroll down the empty halls. Past Maxwell's locker, where we talked about music, and art, and all things of beauty before he betrayed me. Past Ms. Kane's office, where she fed me line after line of feel-good bullshit. Past the auditorium where I first laid eyes on Violet fucking Sarkissian and where my choir was born. None of us speak, each mentally preparing for what is to come, each shaking off the pre-show jitters in our own way.

When we are almost to the gym, just one turn, and maybe thirty yards away, I ask if anyone wants one last drink.

"Why the fuck not?" Asher replies.

I tuck the pistol into my waistband and retrieve my flask from my jacket pocket. I can't get it open with my broken hand, so I hand it to Asher. He lets the M16 hang from its shoulder strap and twists off the cap of the flask. With my gun tucked away, and Asher's hands full, Violet bolts down the hall, toward the gymnasium, crying for help.

J. C. lifts his gun and trains it on her back. I reach out and push his arm down before he can take the shot.

"It's fine," I say. "The first notes are hers to

sing."

We pass the flask around one more time and turn the corner.

CHAPTER 23

Violet is in the doorway of the gym, screaming but really singing. She's not making sense to anyone but us. A teacher and a PTA chaperone stand at the door to the gym, but they don't have ears to hear. Violet's part in the song sounds to them like incoherent screeching. Her bound hands and tear-streaked face leave them unnerved and distracted. They never see us coming.

Violet has had the song to herself for four measures. Now it is time for the rest of us to join in.

Two snare hits are the signal for J. C. and I to begin. My opening note is a middle A and his a middle E. The two adults at the doors crumple and bleed as we sing.

Violet steals a glance back at us as we stride forward. Her eyes are wide with terror, and her flesh is splattered with the blood from the dead chaperones. I have never seen her look so beautiful.

She rushes through purple and gold streamers hanging down from the door frame. Inside a disco ball spins from the ceiling, casting glittery radiance upon the otherwise dim room. She sings her part, and the pop music within cuts out. How could it not?

Violet fucking Sarkissian, for all her flaws, is a showstopper.

She drops my songbook, but that's okay. *The Madrigal* has begun, and it will play out as it must. The world around us is an atonal fantasia, and sometimes art must imitate life.

All eyes are on her, and no one even seems to notice our approach. Some students are coming over, Danny "Fashion Queer" Hammond and Karaoke Joe most notably. They are asking if she's okay, while others put distance between her and themselves, inherently frightened of anything beyond the everyday norm.

We step over the corpses of the grownups in the hall, fallen custodians of a failing society. We walk between the glass cases on either side of the doors, each filled with plastic trophies painted gold—bullshit testaments to bullshit accomplishments. We step through the hanging streamers and into the gymnasium filled with base, faceless people who have all been told that the world is theirs for the taking.

J. C. sings a long note that bends up, then descends into a low boom, at the very bottom of his range. Fire erupts from the gymnasium floor, immolating boys in cheap suits and girls in dresses they can't afford. The flames at the edge of the circle lick at Violet's dress. They embrace her in warmth and radiance, allowing her to shine like never before. She sings her part with such power and volume that her voice carries above the chaos.

Imps, incorporeal things of yellow and orange, drag fleeing students into the burning circle

236

and down into the endless pit below it. Dark smoke rises from the fire and from that smoke the demon forms—a black specter, with the body of a Greek god and the head of a unicorn. It stretches up from the depths of Hell and into the center of the gym. The beast wrestles against burning chains binding it to the pit, as it raises its arms to conduct our performance.

White lights strobe, sirens blare, and steel pipes weep out water upon us. The sprinklers are impotent against the inferno, but the droplets glow like hellish faeries, adding a deeper layer of theatricality to our performance.

I've lost sight of Violet in the chaos of the fire, the panic, and the stagnant rain of the sprinklers, but I hear her. She wails out her part at performance level. Her voice is that of an angel lamenting the burning gates of Heaven.

Asher, so patient and stoic, begins his part in The Madrigal. *His low voice drones out long notes as he pounds out a blast beat of relentless bass and snare. My choir sings as one, and bodies fall around us, each a universe unto itself, now forever extinguished. Brimstone hail rips through arteries and organs. Our voices shatter bone and coax blood from every orifice. All the while, Amduscias, rising from the burning pit below, greedily sups upon death.*

Teachers and students alike flee in rudderless panic. They trample the dead and dying, all pretense of virtue and morality squashed beneath the threat of oblivion. I hope that a few among them might look around before their deaths and see themselves as I do—a gathering of vermin—a writhing ratking.

Amduscias waves his baton toward a group of jocks and burnouts who are throwing themselves against the back door of the gym. Asher turns to them, and their skin sloughs off like shredded meat beneath the sound of his oppressive percussions.

Ms. Kane is ushering students behind an overturned table as if a flimsy bit of molded plastic can save them from the music of Hell. I point toward her, my eyes full of accusation. My expression tells her that this is payback for every fake, paid-for smile she ever cast my way. She shakes her head in a silent plea for mercy.

At the last second I decide to let her live. I want her to bear witness and have to counsel the survivors. I want her to look them in the eyes, and listen to their pain, and know that she could have stopped this if she had only listened.

Instead of ending Ms. Kane's life I turn my attention to the girl standing next to her, one of the cheerleaders who laughed as Ari and his friend dragged me into the bathroom. Kane sees the shift in my gaze and tries to throw herself in front of the girl, but she isn't quick enough.

I sing a sustained whole note, an E at the bottom of my range, and the cheerleader's heart explodes from her chest. Red splatters form sixteenth and double eighth notes in the air that vanish as soon as they are sung.

Ms. Kane grabs the girl in her arms, her face fixed in a scream that's lost below the sound of my choir. She falls to the floor with the cheerleader and presses one hand over the crimson geyser in her chest, as if she can plug her up like a Dutch boy and a dam. The sorrow I see on Ms. Kane's face is the first genuine emotion I have ever witnessed from her. It looks as if we've finally made a breakthrough.

From the corner of my eye, I see movement—something coming my way. Something coming fast. I turn my head, and who do I see but Ari fucking Cole. He's charging over the dead and through the flames to take me out as if he's the hero in all this. That's not going to happen. This story has no heroes, and if it did, it sure as hell wouldn't be Ari Cole.

My voice strikes a discordant note, and Ari's face explodes. His body hits the floor, and the note resolves.

It's a nobler and cleaner death than he deserves. He should have burned to death, cowering among the corpses of his friends. He should have slowly drowned on blood seeping into his lungs, watching my greatest moment in his last.

As we approach the end of The Madrigal, *those blank parts in the score that only the demon knows, a series of timpani strikes sound. They do not come from Asher's drum but from behind me. Noxious smoke rises from the ground in billowy gray clouds. I look up and see Amduscias waving his conductor's wand at something beyond the three of us.*

I turn downstage and see a band of devils with chitinous skin the color of obsidian. They are charging in through the doors of the gymnasium, singing in key with us and beating drums of their own but keeping time with Asher. This is why Amduscias wouldn't give us the entirety of the song. Those blank measures were not ours to perform.

The devils sing to us as we sing to the students of Swift River High, and it becomes clear that we are not immune to the disastrous hymn. Burning hail tears at our flesh and shreds our insides, but our voices stay strong. No one sings too sharp or flat. No one loses time. They've come such a long way, my choir.

Despite the poison smoke choking us, Asher belts out an F, twice below middle C, an accompaniment to my sustained D sharp, and plays a rapid snare roll that fills the air with atomized gore. At the end of the roll he goes silent and falls.

J. C. trills wildly between A and C. The sound of his voice echoes off the closed bleachers, then he too stops singing, a single measure after Asher.

It's just me now. I don't know where Violet is or if she's dead or alive. I can't hear her voice, but maybe her part is over and she's found cover somewhere. Or maybe she's smoldering, dead on the floor. It doesn't really matter, I suppose.

The devils are still playing their drums, and some organ bursts behind my ribs. I'm dying. Of that there's no doubt. The song is nearly complete, however, and I will sing until this body fails.

I throw my arms out to my sides, with operatic drama. With everything left in me I finish the final measure, my tone and power never wavering. I give the world this final gift, a triumphant cadenza and a perfect cadence, as I toss myself back into the flames.

Wild agony engulfs my being. My skin blisters and chars, and my heart stops. Clawed hands take hold of me with the strength of a black hole, but even as Amduscias, my muse and betrayer, drags me down into the depths of Hell I have no fear. I shall be immortal in my art, the best parts of me captured in stave and song. Neither death nor Hell can undo that magic.

ABOUT THE AUTHOR

Curtis M. Lawson is an author of unapologetically weird and transgressive fiction, fantastical graphic novels, and dark poetry. Curtis' work ranges from technicolor pulp adventures to bleak cosmic horror. Curtis is a member of the Horror Writer's Association, and the organizer of the *Wyrd* live horror reading series. He lives in Salem, MA with his wife and their son.

Black Heart Boys' Choir Playlist

One of the most rewarding aspects of writing this story was the journey I took through the world of classical music. Below is a list of works referenced in this book. Countless other pieces contributed to my writing soundtrack, but this is a nice place to start for anyone who might want to chase this incredible music down the proverbial rabbit hole.

Ludwig van Beethoven -
Symphony No. 9 in D minor
Bagatelle No. 25 in A minor for solo piano - Für Elise

J. S. Bach -
Mass in B minor

Samuel Barber-
Agnus Dei

William Byrd -
Mass for Four Voices

Frederic Chopin -
Nocturne in E Flat major, Op. 9 No. 2

Glenn Danzig -
Black Aria

Claude Debussy -
Clair de Lune

Ludovico Einaudi -

Nuvole Bianche

Henryk Gorecki -
Symohony No. 3, Op. 36 - Symphony of
Sorrowful Songs

Wolfgang Amadeus Mozart -
Piano Sonata No. 16 in C major, K. 545 - Sonata
Facile

Nicolo Paganini -
24 caprices

Pyotr Ilyich Tchaikovsky -
Marche Slave in B flat minor, Op. 31

Tomas Luis de Victoria -
O Magnum Mysterium

Richard Wagner -
Das Rheingold

Made in the USA
Monee, IL
03 March 2020

22623898R10150